F. G. Trafford

George Geith of Fen Court

Vol. 2

SALZWASSER
VERLAG

F. G. Trafford

George Geith of Fen Court

Vol. 2

Reprint of the original, first published in 1864.

1st Edition 2022 | ISBN: 978-3-75259-385-3

Verlag (Publisher): Salzwasser Verlag GmbH, Zeilweg 44, 60439 Frankfurt, Deutschland
Vertretungsberechtigt (Authorized to represent): E. Roepke, Zeilweg 44, 60439 Frankfurt, Deutschland
Druck (Print): Books on Demand GmbH, In de Tarpen 42, 22848 Norderstedt, Deutschland

GEORGE GEITH OF FEN COURT.

VOL II.

GEORGE GEITH

OF

FEN COURT

𝔄 𝔑𝔬𝔳𝔢𝔩.

By F. G. TRAFFORD

IN THREE VOLUMES.

VOL. II.

LONDON

1864.

CONTENTS.

CHAPTER I.

PAGE

AT THE DOWER HOUSE 1

CHAPTER II.

QUITE AT HOME 23

CHAPTER III.

HAPPINESS 48

CHAPTER IV.

BERYL'S ADMIRER 66

CHAPTER V.

BERYL EXPLAINS 86

CHAPTER VI.

ACROSS THE FIELDS 102

CHAPTER VII.

A LITTLE SURPRISE 125

CHAPTER VIII.

MR. RICHARD ELSENHAM 142

CHAPTER IX.

BACK TO TOWN 158

PAGE

CHAPTER X.

DAY DREAMS 180

CHAPTER XI.

ALTERNATIONS 190

CHAPTER XII.

CHRISTMAS EVE 203

CHAPTER XIII.

DOMESTIC PERPLEXITIES 218

CHAPTER XIV.

DEATH 241

CHAPTER XV.

EAVESDROPPING 251

CHAPTER XVI.

IN LONDON 283

CHAPTER XVII.

PLEASANT HOURS 297

GEORGE GEITH OF FEN COURT.

CHAPTER I.

AT THE DOWER HOUSE.

ON the whole, George Geith was very glad when
the day arrived for him to revisit Withefell. He
said to himself that it was a confounded bore to
have to leave all his town business, to go poking
into the entangled affairs of a country gentleman
who could not trust his papers into the hands of
a stranger; but still George was glad, for if he had
not wanted to go, he could have declined the
work.

As it was, he accepted the work, and went down
to the Dower House to finish it.

Finishing, however, did not in this case prove
nearly so easy as beginning; and before George
Geith had been three hours engaged at Mr.

Molozane's papers, he found he should either be a loser by the transaction, or have to charge his employer an exorbitant price.

It was one of those pieces of business which he was in the habit of taking in town and doing at his leisure; when no person's books wanted balancing, no man's schedule haunted his sleep.

No money could pay him for going down to Withefell, and setting Mr. Molozane's house in order. Was it possible for him to devise any plan by which he might do at once justice to the Squire and himself? Could he leave town every night and sleep at Wattisbridge for a month? Could he re-establish his health and get through Mr. Molozane's business at one and the same time?

If the gentleman would wait his convenience, George thought the thing might be managed; and accordingly he broached the subject whilst he and the Squire were wading together through the accounts.

"As you like," answered Mr. Molozane. "I am in no hurry to know the worst. Providing the thing be done, I am not particular as to when, only you must stay here; you must consider this your inn for the time being."

"But," expostulated George, "when I am making this arrangement solely to suit my own convenience——"

"I presume I may make an arrangement to suit my own pleasure likewise," finished Mr. Molozane. "We will just settle the matter at once, Mr. Geith. Come when you like, go when you like, finish when you like."

And thus George Geith was made free of the Dower House, and soon became quite one of the family.

Looking back, he could not believe his host to be one and the same, with the man who had walked into his office nine months before with such a haughty mien, with such unconciliating manners. He could not identify Mr. Molozane at home with Mr. Molozane abroad. He could not understand how the fences had come to be broken down between them; how Mr. Molozane could regard absolutely in the light of a friend one whom he had once treated somewhat as a servant.

The accountant could not know that Mr. Molozane felt this silent, untiring, clear-headed, hard-working man ought to be able to keep the evil to come away from his threshold, or, if that were impossible, would tell him how best the evil might be met.

He was so thankful to have an adviser, a helper, a man who, mentally, was a self-reliant giant, that he ran to extremes in the matter; and thought in George's presence there was safety; in his absence, danger.

Besides, he liked his new acquaintance better than any friend or neighbour he possessed.

He could talk to George without the necessity for constant concealment; he could be silent without exciting remark; he could be worse than silent—dull, and still the accountant knew the why and the wherefore, and was not surprised.

Further, though Mr. Geith was in business, he yet possessed the manners and feelings of a gentleman. How he had come by those manners and feelings, Mr. Molozane did not know, and George did not enlighten him; but they were pleasant to the Squire for all that; and he took this new acquaintance into favour, without stopping to consider why he did so, or how the intimacy might end.

He liked George and made him welcome; and George liked his quarters, and made himself at home. For a time, of course, the accountant went through the ceremony of deceiving himself, of mentally saying it was a bore to have to leave town, a nuisance having to relinquish paying work for unremunerative; but after a very little he grew honest, and acknowledged that his life just then was a pleasanter existence than it had been for years.

It was more cheerful, certainly, for no place could be dull in which Beryl Molozane abode; and as he got more and more at home, so Beryl unveiled before him, and showed this old man of the world what he had never seen before—a perfectly natural light-hearted girl. Who was as bright as the sunshine, as gay as a kitten; who thought no more what anyone thought about her, than if she had been only three years old; who took Mr. Geith into her confidence, and made the Dower House a home to the homeless man.

By degrees, too, Miss Molozane's ice thawed, and she began to treat George with such favour, as showed she had ceased to think of him as an accountant, and had come to understand he was a man.

Whilst for Louey, she made no secret of her

liking, but said openly, and in the face of the family congregation, she thought Mr. Geith nicer than anybody she knew, Mr. Werne not excepted. And, up to this point, I may remark, Mr. Werne, of Molozane Park, had been the god of the young lady's idolatry.

To work in that house was not easy; to work the whole day through, a thing not to be dreamed of; and with dismay George saw that the progress he was making was of the slowest.

Very conscientiously he pointed this out to Mr. Molozane, and entreated permission to take the papers with him to town; but this the Squire would not allow.

Perhaps he saw from George's manner that he was by no means loth to stay; that he found the country air beneficial; that the mental atmosphere he was breathing seemed pleasanter and purer than all. Anyhow, he entreated him not to trouble himself; to come when he could, to stay away when it was more convenient, and to be satisfied Mr. Molozane was very glad for him to remain, and should be very sorry when he had to go.

Thus it came to pass that the accountant grew more and more intimate with every member of the family; that he shared their merriment, knew their anxieties, and began to understand what home really was.

"Should he ever feel happy away from one again?" the lonely man asked himself, whilst leaning out of his window, looking at the Park as it lay bathed in the silvery moonlight. "Am I wise?" he thought; "am I safe?" and he sat down and pictured Matilda Molozane and her beauty till he concluded he was not safe, that he ought to depart at all hazards.

Then he ran on to other matters; all, however, connected with her. Why was she better dressed, better mounted, better cared for, than anyone else about the house? How did it happen that, in spite of the close economy practised in the house, an economy which the Molozanes were either too proud or too frank to endeavour to conceal from him, the beauty seemed to know no lack of anything? For Beryl and Louey, muslins and prints, bonnets apparently home trimmed; mantles he himself had seen Beryl making! For Miss Molozane, the richest of dresses, the most fashionable of bonnets, the most delicate of gloves.

Except good wine and heavy plate, there was

nothing, in or about the house, such as might have
been expected in the home of a man who still held
a good position in the county, and was known for
miles round as " the Squire." The furniture, though
handsome, was old; the curtains were faded; the
carpets threadbare.   There were but two female
servants and one man about the establishment;
and as for the table, the fare satisfied George, who
was not particular; but many a London shop-
keeper would have turned up his nose in contempt,
at the plainness of the fare with which the Molozanes were perfectly content.

It was not that the viands were ill-cooked, or
badly served: it was merely that at every turn
economy was practised, and that luxuries of all
kinds, the speculative but conscientious gentleman
eschewed.

And there were signs and tokens also which
proved that this economy was not a matter of
recent growth; that Beryl had told him the literal
truth when she said one day:

"I have never known what it is to have money
all my life, Mr. Geith.   We have been short of it
ever since I can remember anything."

She said it laughingly, making light of her little

domestic anxieties; but George remembered the sentence, and puzzled himself about the apparent incongruity there existed, between Miss Molozane's belongings and her father's means.

Almost as if she had guessed what was passing in his mind, Beryl came to him next morning, when he was standing on the lawn, watching the groom exercising her sister's horse, and said, with a slight flush on her cheek—

"I have often thought, Mr. Geith, that horse must puzzle you; but perhaps you know it is not ours: it is Mrs. Elsenham's. Mrs. Elsenham is that delightful old grandmother about whom you have heard me talk."

"Would it be impertinent for me to inquire why Mrs. Elsenham does not provide a horse for you likewise?"

"Certainly not. I shall be delighted to tell you about Granny, because I hate her. It is a comfort to meet with any person to whom I can say fearlessly, 'I detest my grandmother!' And I give you fair warning, Mr. Geith, that if you say it is wrong of me to do so, I shall hate you too."

"Then assuredly, whatever I may think, I shall keep a discreet silence," he answered.

" But you must not think; at least, you must not think differently from what I do. Granny is the most detestable old woman that ever lived! The first time Tilly is out of the way, I will show you Granny exact. She and I have been at daggers drawn since I can remember anything."

" And is that the reason she does not let you have a horse?" asked George, anxious to draw her back to the point whence they had started.

" Not at all: the reason of that is—but I think I must begin at the beginning, and tell you a little piece of our family history. I do not see why you should not know what all the parish knows, a great deal better than its alphabet."

" I have no claim to be told anything, however, Miss Beryl," remarked George, virtuously.

" I never said you had; but I should like to tell you; and then, no matter what you see about the house, you will not be astonished. Papa would tell you only that it is a sore subject; for he hates Granny more than I do. She took him in; she cheated him, in plain words, Mr. Geith. But for Granny, we should have been still up at the Park, and I should never have been talking to you here."

If she expected her companion to regret this, she was mistaken. Perhaps she did not: at all events, she proceeded:

" I should tell you, Mr. Geith, that I scarcely remember my mother at all. Indeed, I question if I should recollect her, but that my memory has always been refreshed by that portrait which hangs between the dining-room windows. She must have been very like Matilda, I think. Papa says she was handsomer, but I scarcely can imagine that. You think Tilly very handsome, don't you, Mr. Geith?"

Was this chit of seventeen trying him? Did she want to ascertain whether he cared too much for her sister or not? Had she guessed he stood in danger? Was she warning him off the track?

All this passed through George Geith's mind as he answered, with an amused smile, that he did consider Miss Molozane very beautiful — more beautiful even, in his opinion, than the portrait in the dining-room.

" Thank you, Mr. Geith," said Beryl, simply; and she thought for a moment before she went on. " After all, it is not so easy to tell a story," was her next sentence, and she laughed and coloured at her own awkwardness. " In some respects it is

not a pleasant story, and that makes it more difficult for me to know what part to put first. Before
papa came into the Park, it was mortgaged; but
everybody thought his wife's fortune would more
than set him straight. You must have heard of
Mr. Elsenham, who made such a gigantic fortune
out of Bandana handkerchiefs. He was my grandfather; and as he had but two children, a son and
daughter, people said papa would be better off
than any Molozane had been for centuries.

"During his lifetime Mr. Elsenham would make
no settlement on my mother. He allowed her
six hundred a year, and he used to give her splen-
did presents (we have some of her jewellery now);
and it was an understood thing that when he died
she was to have a third of his property. When he
did die, however, it turned out that his wife (that's
Granny, you understand) had got him to leave
every halfpenny under her control. She was a lady
who liked power, and everything was, for the future,
in her power. I do not say the disappointment
killed my mother, but it certainly hastened her
death. She died when Louey was born, and then
Granny stopped the allowance altogether, and has
kept it to herself ever since."

"Do you mean, Mr. Molozane never had any part of his wife's fortune—that Mrs. Elsenham has made no arrangement about you?"

"Oh! she has arranged!—I was going to tell you about that," replied Beryl. My uncle Harry died before his father, leaving one son. This son, Richard, has been brought up by his grandmother, who is going to do great things for him; and she proposed, years and years ago, that Dick should marry Matilda, and the money be thus kept in the family."

"And Mr. Molozane?" asked George.

"Papa did what was right, as you might be quite sure he would," answered Beryl, whose cheeks were by this time crimson. "He would not have Matilda bound by any such engagement, till she was old enough to decide for herself. And Matilda has decided, and they will be married whenever Richard comes of age."

For a minute there was silence. With all his self-command George could not make an indifferent remark on the subject; and had he been more at ease himself, Beryl's visible embarrassment would have rendered it difficult for him to know what to say.

They had wandered, during their conversation, from the lawn to a walk which wound away by the side of the Park, and Beryl was now leaning on the oak paling that separated her old home from her present one, with her face buried in her hands.

Was she crying? and, if she were, what was the cause of her grief? Had she cared for this cousin? Had there been any quarrel between her sister and herself? Was it the old, old story, of young people thrown together, of hearts exchanged without permission, of an engagement being forbidden, of a union proving impossible? Was this young thing, gay as she seemed, really in trouble? Had she been called on to give up, without a murmur, all the hopes of her life? And was she, now in the very spring and promise of her existence, weeping over withered flowers?

Thinking this, there came a dangerous longing into George Geith's heart to comfort her, to tell her what he knew about life; to assure her that so long as men and women will battle against grief for themselves, so long, likewise, God in his mercy permits the sun to rise for them after the darkest nights of misery and despair humanity knows.

Many a word which he could not have spoken in

the days when he was a clergyman, when consolation was his office, comfort his business, he
would willingly have poured out then. Many a
sentence which he had learned out of the great
lesson book that the Almighty opens for us all,
clerical or lay, occurred to him then; but he was
wise, and held his peace. There was nothing in
what Beryl had told to warrant observation from
him; and although he felt, or fancied he felt, at the
moment, the same longing to comfort the girl as a
father might to comfort his vexed child, he luckily
remembered he was not her father, and Beryl not
a child.

"You know now," she went on after that pause,
uncovering her face, but still not looking at him,
but letting her eyes, wet with tears, wander out
over the Park, "you know now why Matilda has
everything different from us. It is not her fault,
for Granny insists that the future Mrs. Elsenham
shall have all that befits her station. I should have
thought," added Beryl, with a fire in her eyes
which seemed to dry the moisture out of them in
an instant, "that a Molozane needed as much as
an Elsenham, any day; but I suppose gentry can
afford to do without things that *parvenus* cannot.

My sister must have that horse and groom; my sister must be dressed like Solomon in all his glory; whilst Louey and I are simple as the lilies of the field. Would I do it?" and Beryl clenched her little hand. "Would I do the bidding of any old woman? Would I be a slave for the sake of any amount of money that could be offered to me?"

She was so vehement that, for the life of him, George could not help laughing, even whilst he answered:

"Perhaps you would not be a slave for the sake of money; but you might, for the sake of some one you cared for very much?"

"I do not think I should; but, at any rate, it would not be for the sake of Dick Elsenham. You will see him to-night, and a very nice kind of person you will see, if you are not at all particular."

"Why, what kind of person may he be?" asked George.

"He is this," said Beryl, pulling off her bonnet, and running her fingers through her hair: "and he is this," and she stroked an imaginary moustache: "and he is this," and she caressed her soft cheek: "and he is this," and she drawled out her words with an affected lisp: "and he is this," and George absolutely started at the sudden insolence and assurance of her manner: "and he is this," and she drew back like a sullen coward: "he is a fop; he is a fool; he is a bully; he is—to be my brother-in-law," and Beryl lifted up her head like a young war-horse scenting the battle afar off.

"Is there no help for it?" George inquired.

"Yes, if you can give us back the Park free from mortgages; if you can give us horses, carriages, servants; beyond all things, money," she scoffed. "Mr. Geith, you must not think Matilda mad, when you see Richard. She has been with my grandmother most part of her life—off and on, I mean—and she cannot endure what we can. Short means are a wretchedness to her. She has always been accustomed to have everything she wants. She likes gaiety. It would be a living death to her to have to stay here always. Besides, she does not dislike Richard as I do. She likes him. If she did not—if it were only for the money she was marrying—I know a man that, were I in her place, I would chose before Dick, twenty times over. I had rather hear his grammar than Dick's drawl. I should prefer his stories to Dick's oaths. You will hear Mr. Richard Elsenham swearing, morning, noon, and night; but you must never mind him, Mr. Geith; no matter what he says or does."

George bit his lip; he was coming now to an understanding of what the young lady desired—of what she was entreating at his hands.

" Would it not be better for me to go ?" he asked ; " and return when Mr. Elsenham leaves ?"

" I do not know when you would return, then," she answered ; " for he lives here nine months out of the twelve. Either here or at Wattisbridge, I mean," she added, " which is much the same thing."

" I wonder if Mr. Molozane would allow me to take the necessary papers to town ?" he said.

" Do not ask him ; pray do not," she entreated. " If you knew what a comfort it is to papa to have anybody to talk to whilst Dick is here, you would never think of going. Besides, if you begin with my cousin as you mean to go on, you will have no trouble ; only you must not mind him, even though he should be tiresome sometimes."

He made no answer till they had paced the whole length of the walk, and were almost at the house again. Then he said :

" Is it to be peace at any price, Miss Beryl ?"

"If you can manage it, Mr. Geith, I shall be very grateful."

" Then I will try," he said ; and the girl left him and ran in.

Just then, out came Miss Molozane in her riding-habit; with her coquetish hat and drooping feather ; with her light riding-whip and her flowing veil. She was looking for George to help her to mount. It was a duty he had taken kindly to ; and, to say the truth, Miss Molozane did not object to the attention in the least.

There were so many folds in the habit to be properly arranged ; there was so much nicety required about the curb ; the reins were so often twisted ; and the girths needed such close inspection, that this business of mounting had come to be quite a serious affair ; a something which occupied a long time, and gave opportunity for a considerable amount of innocent flirtation.

On the occasion in question, as George knoted up the curb rein to the particular length desired by the fair equestrian ; as he patted the arched neck of the beautiful animal she rode, a thought passed through his mind as to whether he should declare boldly to her who he was, and try to go in and win this prize.

c 2

But, pooh! what chance had he? What was
his birth in comparison to Elsenham's money?
what his possibilities beside Elsenham's certainties?
and, even if he had a chance, were these grapes
worth climbing after?

They were very nice to look at; but George did
not know much about how they would taste as
a form of refreshment for life. He had his doubts;
he was not a young man in feelings, ideas, or
even age, you remember, my reader; and though
he seemed to have taken a fresh lease of youth
at the Dower House, he had still his experience
of former tendencies to fall back on, in case
of need. He rather thought Miss Molozane
might not be worth the trouble; and already the
fancy he had felt was passing away from him as
quickly almost as the lady was disappearing down
the avenue.

"She rides well, don't she, sir?" said a voice close
beside him; and turning, he beheld Mr. Molozane's
factotum, groom, gardener, coachman, standing at
his elbow. Standing with a cloth in his hand,
with which cloth he was in the habit of giving a
finishing polish to any bit, buckle, or stirrup, that
might seem to stand in need of such attention.

"I taught her, I did; when master lived at the Park, I taught her. It was me first held her on a pony. Yes, she do ride well; and that's a nice thing she's on. Mr. Elsenham, he rides well too. "They make a handsome pair, they do; but I know, if I was a gentleman, which I would choose. I'd never take Miss Molozane whilst Miss Beryl was single: and I've known them both since they was as high as my knee, I have."

"Does Miss Beryl never ride at all?" asked George, as much perhaps in order to turn the conversation as from any desire for information.

"Not often; her pony can't hold foot with the chestnut. When Mr. Elsenham is here, he sometimes gets her to try one of his horses, but Miss Beryl is afraid now. He has served her such tricks, she is afraid of being thrown. He says he wants to make her sure of her seat; but I know better. It is just his jokes," muttered the old man, as he shuffled away; adding something under his breath, which was not, George suspected, a blessing on Mr. Richard Elsenham.

"I'd like to catch the fellow playing any tricks with her," thought the accountant, as he sat down in the library, and commenced sorting over the papers: "I'd duck him in the nearest horse-pond."

From which expression it will be seen that the promise of peace at any price Beryl had exacted from her new friend, was not altogether unnecessary or uncalled for.

CHAPTER II.

QUITE AT HOME.

WHEN a young lady has, from the age of fifteen, been in the habit of managing her father's house, directing his servants, and making arrangements for the reception of his guests, her manners naturally become formed much earlier than would have been the case under ordinary circumstances. More particularly if the said young lady have from her earliest infancy been deprived of maternal guidance; and freed from that constant contemplation of what is proper and improper, which it seems the especial province of mothers to force upon the consideration of their daughters.

It may be rank heresy, but I hold to the belief nevertheless, that if girls be nice at all, they are nicer when they are allowed to grow up with their feet out of the stocks, and their figures free from backboards.

It is pleasant to see a young girl starting in life without picking her steps too much; and young ladies who know all the pitfalls and quagmires of this wicked world, are apt to lose in simplicity what they gain in propriety.

Mothers wise in their generation, who are acquainted with the evil, and the sin, and the sorrow, are so anxious to keep their girls from the appearance of evil, that they will not suffer them to be natural. They forget, God help us, what one would think they ought to remember with thankfulness, that there is a time, when it is as natural to the young to be frank and open as it seems to be afterwards to the old, to be masked and veiled. They will not let well alone. They will have every word, look, action, ruled by line and plummet. They leave nothing to impulse, because, as I have said before, they forget there is a time when impulses are not all sinful, when it is natural to the young to laugh and be glad as it is to the lark to sing.

Which brings me back to what I meant to say at first, viz., that George Geith thought Beryl

Molozane would not have been half so pleasant a girl had she been brought up under the eye of the stately beauty whose portrait hung in the dining-room.

He knew no mother would have suffered Beryl to wander through life at her own sweet will in the manner Mr. Molozane permitted. But still Mr. Geith had very sincere doubts as to whether a more properly trained young lady might not have plunged headlong into errors which Beryl avoided. She was no flirt—she never appeared embarrassed. George had seen a good deal of the world, and he had certainly never been in a house where there seemed more union amongst the members of the family, and from which the mystery and wickedness of ordinary life was better excluded. Between Beryl and her father, indeed, there existed such perfect sympathy, such a thorough understanding, that George felt sure the girl would do nothing, say nothing, think nothing, which she would hesitate to confess to her parent on the spot. Indeed, in this way Beryl was a little provoking; because once or twice when she had talked to him, as George in his vanity thought, confidentially, he was astonished afterwards to find her repeating almost the same sentences in her father's presence, without the slightest idea that she was disappointing one of her auditors.

A girl who took this new acquaintance into her confidence, just as if she had known him all her life; who talked before him about her slightest housekeeping troubles; who mimicked their acquaintances, hitting off each person's oddities with a dangerous power of mockery; whom he would meet in unexpected places laughing till the tears ran down her cheeks; who was like a kitten, everywhere at once; who was not a young lady, nor even a girl, but just a child in everything save the power of keeping the house in order, and of making things comfortable for those about her; a merry drudge; a laughing Grisel, whom the servants loved as very few servants love any mistress now-a-days: how could a man help liking this young thing, thinking of her, speculating about her future?

Whom would she marry? Would she settle down into respectable matronhood, and become quite another creature in the space of a very few years?

Would she marry a rich man, or a poor?

Would she ever become fashionable, ever learn concealment, ever become different to what she then was? Somehow, George found her future impossible even to picture. He could not fancy Time's hand laid on her—always young, always laughing, he could imagine her going singing away through life; but he could not imagine her changing— becoming cold, worldly, calculating.

Thinking of the girl, now laughing inwardly at the recollection of some queer speech, some expression of anger; now remembering all her unselfishness, all her devotion, George found he was making very little progress with his accounts, and that if he was ever to get them finished he must stay more in the library, and not permit himself to be so frequently beguiled into leaving that retreat for the pleasanter sitting-room of the family.

So to work he went in earnest; toiling through the long hours of that summer day, labouring with the windows open, and every external sight, and sound, and perfume, tempting him out into the open air. He would not leave off even for luncheon— the pleasant meal which had always hitherto made such a delightful break in the hours, when he had spent a whole day at the Dower House.

To be sure, he did not gain much by the move, for Beryl herself brought him what he asked for—biscuits and water; called him unsociable, an anchorite, a hermit, and then went and gathered him fruit, which she laid on the table, nestling amongst the leaves of the mulberry and the vine.

Fruit is not a thing which even anchorites find it easy to resist. Fruit cannot be eaten like biscuits, with pen in hand and eye on paper, for both which reasons George was obliged to cease from labour and talk whilst he refreshed himself. Then Mr. Molozane came in, and settled down ostensibly to read the paper, but really, as it seemed, to hinder George getting on with his business. Nevertheless, he did make considerable progress, and would have worked right on till it was time to dress for dinner, but that at about five o'clock Beryl appeared at one of the front windows opening on to the terrace, entreating him to cease writing before he grew into a machine.

"How you can go, on, on, hour after hour, I cannot imagine," said this steady young woman. "How you can live out of the sunshine, away from the flowers, puzzles me. Why, even Louey leaves her manuscripts; she is here now. Do come out; I wish you would."

"We shan't be able to enjoy ourselves much longer," observed Louisa, who had a wide-brimmed straw hat tied over her cap. "When once Dick comes we shall soon have his grandmother, and then there will be a pleasant houseful."

"I always enjoy myself when Granny is here," said Beryl. "I don't know when I have greater fun."

"Because you are always mimicking her. Mr. Geith, Beryl walks into the room behind grand-mamma, on tiptoe, mocking her all the time; she has been nearly caught, over and over again; indeed she was once, for Granny saw her in the glass."

"I wonder if I dare," said Beryl, looking round. "Louey, is Matilda out of the way? Now, Mr. Geith, here is Granny;" and Beryl, gathering up her dress in both hands, straightening her back till it was as flat as a table, drawing up her neck, and stiffening her limbs, sailed up and down the terrace with all the pomp and majesty of an ancient lady, till George, fairly overcome by the ludicrous contrast between Beryl and the woman she was making believe to be, had to sit down on one of the terrace seats, where he laughed, as he had not laughed before for years.

"May I inquire, sir, what is amusing you so much?" said Beryl, stopping short in her walk, and asking the question in her grandmother's very voice.

Then, "Oh, my gracious goodness! here is Tilly. Well, Matilda, and how are you?" And she went sailing up to her sister, and bestowed upon her a most impressive salute.

"Beryl, how can you?" exclaimed the beauty. "What will Mr. Geith think? How can you be so absurd?"

"I am only moulding myself after a most desirable model," answered Beryl, still in her cracked, old woman's voice; "and Mr. Geith or any other mister may think what he pleases. When I am in the path of duty, the remarks of the herd fail to affect me in the least. I suppose Maria Elsenham may walk up and down her own terraced walks without drawing down the impertinent comments of strangers."

And Beryl was off again, sweeping, rustling as she went.

"I ought not to laugh, Miss Molozane, I know," said George, apologetically.

" For once, Mr. Geith, you have arrived at a just conclusion," remarked Beryl, severely, as she moved past.

" It is not possible to help laughing at Beryl," said Miss Molozane; " that is the worst of it; and our laughing encourages her to do, and say things she would never otherwise dream of. You know, Mr. Geith, she ought not to mimic her grandmother, and——"

" Once for all, young woman," interrupted Beryl, tapping her on the shoulder with a gesture George knew must have been copied from life; " once for all, young woman, understand that *I* did not choose *my* grandmother, and that I maintain I have a right to mimic her if I choose. *You* may have chosen *your* grandmother, and, if so, I do not think much of your taste; let that settle the question, there." And Beryl opened and shut her eyes once or twice imperatively, and balanced herself on her heels, much as a parrot balances itself on its perch.

" You will get us all into some frightful scrape," observed Miss Molozane, dolefully.

In a moment Beryl dropped her grandmother, and was her own proper self again.

" How shall I get you into a scrape ?" she asked.

" Can Granny kill us ? Can she send us to the Tower ? Is she our queen ? are we her subjects ? Does she pay our debts ? Does she do anything but make herself as disagreeable as she knows how when she comes down here ? Get into a scrape ! I wish I could keep her out of the house by getting into a scrape, that I do !—yes, that I do !" And Miss Beryl's cheeks flamed, while she stamped her little foot on the ground, to add emphasis to her words.

" But would it not be wise to cease talking about her when she is not here ?" asked her sister.

" Do you want me to go into a thousand pieces when she is here ?" asked Beryl. " Do you want me to explode with pent-up wrath and indignation ? Should you like to see me in bits—a leg here and an arm there ? If so, you will tell me to hold my peace about Granny. If I could not say I hated her, I should die ; but as it is, the thought of the fun I can make of her enables me to behave with civility when she is in the house. You do not know how civil I am to Granny, Mr. Geith ; and she can't bear my civility or me either."

" And she can't endure me," put in Louey.

"But you wrote a poem about her," said Beryl.
"She did, indeed; and, as it happened, the poem
got into Matilda's desk, which she lent one day to
Granny. Matilda is excessively ready to lend things
to Granny, I may remark; and the delightful old
lady looking for note-paper, she says—but, as I
believe, rummaging for secrets—came on this poem,
and read it, and had us all in and interrogated us,
and sent for papa; and we had such a to-do. The
poem began—

> "At Kensington there dwells a dame,
> Maria Elsenham is her name,
> And ——"

"Beryl, I desire you to stop," broke in Miss
Molozane. "Mr. Geith, you might tell her how
wrong it is. Perhaps she will listen to what you
say, though she will not attend to me."

"Miss Beryl, I really do think," began George,
but she interrupted him with—

"You need not go on. I know all you are
going to say much better than you do yourself.
You were wanting to tell me about grey hairs and
young heads. You were about to say that Granny
must be a lady of the highest respectability
and wealth; and that my conduct amounts to

sacrilege. You were going to tell me the fate of those children who mocked Elisha; and to inform me that people who ridicule others are often ridiculed themselves: but it is of no use. No matter what is right or what is wrong, I must laugh at Granny; and for anything else I don't care."

"Do you know what happened to 'don't care?'" asked Miss Molozane.

"There have been so many 'don't cares,'" retorted Beryl. "There was one ran away to sea and was drowned; one fell among savages; one was eaten by a lion on the coast of Africa (I would tell you what part of the coast, only I don't know that myself); and another happened to have a sister called Matilda. Her fate was the hardest of all, I think—but I hear horse's hoofs; I hear Sultan trotting up the drive; and I know Dick is coming, and I am not dressed to receive him. There, Miss Matty, that is your fault—there." And Beryl pulled a grimace.

"Do you know whether papa is in the house?" asked Miss Molozane, who coloured perceptibly at Beryl's intelligence.

"I don't know, and I don't care," murmured that young lady. "Dick will be sure to find us out. I am not going to meet him, Tilly, if that is what you are looking so pitiful about. If you think it necessary for any one to ask him to make himself at home, you can go and do so yourself."

" We had better go in," suggested Miss Molozane.

"Not at all; I am very comfortable where I am. Ah! here he comes;" and at that instant George heard the library door flung open; then an audible "Where the devil are they all!" which sentence was immediately followed by the speaker, who stepped out on to the terrace and greeted his cousins with—

" Well, girls, how are you?"

" We feel a great deal better now you are come," answered Beryl, demurely; and she held out her hand to the young man, who evidently considered that his relationship justified a warmer salutation, which he might have exacted, but that at the moment he caught sight of Mr. Geith.

There was a supercilious lifting of his eyebrows, a contemptuous measuring of the stranger's social standing, an unqualified stare of amazement; and then a look towards Beryl which said as plainly as a look could, " Who the deuce is this fellow, and what is he doing here?"

"Mr. Elsenham, Mr. Geith," Beryl answered; and thereupon the two gentlemen bowed.

"You must have found it very warm riding this afternoon," remarked the accountant.

"Infernally," was the reply; and Mr. Elsenham took off his hat as he spoke.

"You are covered with dust," said Louisa, with the air of a person who considered she had made an original observation.

"These cursed roads are always dusty," Mr. Elsenham graciously answered.

"Most roads are so when they are not muddy," opined Louisa, at which speech the young man laughed.

"Have you written any proverbs since I saw you last, Solomon?" he asked. "No! Nor finished ten tragedies; nor made a better Paradise than Milton's? You lazy little wretch! I'll see that you work whilst I am here. And when are you going to get rid of that cap. I give you fair notice I shall set it on fire;" and he was making a step towards the girl, when Beryl interrupted him.

"I won't have it, Richard," she said. "You shall not torment Louey. Let her cap alone, and her too."

"It is such an outrageous thing," he observed.

"Nobody asks you to wear it," she retorted; and then the idea of Dick in a cap so overcame her, that Miss Molozane felt constrained to interfere and rebuke her sister severely.

"Know this part of the country well?" asked Mr. Elsenham, turning towards Mr. Geith.

"No, it is quite strange to me; and I am not likely to know it much better, for I am only here on business."

"Humph," grunted Mr. Elsenham, and he took a comprehensive glance round the party; after which he said, "that business must be a d——d bore, though, thank the Lord, he knew nothing about it save by report."

"It is lucky for you that your grandfather had a closer acquaintance with it," remarked Miss Beryl.

"It is well there are some people in the world who will work like galley slaves," answered Mr. Elsenham. "I'll be hanged if I would."

"Would you rather starve, Dick?" asked Louisa; whereupon the young man told her to "shut up;" and inquired if Mr. Geith would have "a weed."

The politeness being declined, Mr. Elsenham lit a cigar for himself, and asked where his uncle was.

"He is gone to the Park, I think," answered Miss Molozane; upon receiving which information, her cousin at once turned to Beryl with—

"And how is Mr. Werne?"

"So far as I know, he is quite well," she replied.

"And how far do you know?" he asked, taking the cigar out of his mouth, and putting the question in a tone, which George by no means approved.

"The last time papa was at the Park, he made no mention of Mr. Werne being ill. As you seem particularly interested about him, however, perhaps I had better send Robert up to inquire."

"I'm not interested in the fellow, hang him! I don't care a d——d sixpence whether he is ill or well. Have you seen this Withefell saint, Mr. Geith? And what do you think of him?"

"I have not seen him," answered the accountant, "nor heard of him, save from Miss Louisa."

"You should get Beryl at the bellows then. Who is wise, holy, good? Mr. Werne. Who is well-informed, well-bred, well-travelled? Mr. Werne. Who never swears, never is out of temper, never d——s his servants? Mr. Werne. And, if I may add so much on my own account, who is the most cursed hypocrite, the most confounded upstart, the most intolerable prig? Mr. Werne!"

"It would be a blessing for us if you were only like him, instead of being what you are — a slanderer of a good man, before whom you dare not say the things you say before us!" panted Beryl.

"Ah! Mr. Geith, that is all very fine, but don't let it impose upon you. Beryl abuses me in company, but you cannot imagine all the nice compliments she pays when we are alone;" and Mr. Elsenham puffed a cloud of smoke out of his mouth, and watched it curling up into the silent air.

If ever Mr. Geith felt a desire to kick a man, it was at that moment. He would have liked to thrash the fellow, and thrust him neck-and-crop off the premises. He longed to pick a quarrel with him, to get an opportunity of telling this new comer what he thought of him, his manners, and his speeches; but he luckily remembered his promise to Beryl, and biting back his words, kept peace.

"You are fortunate," he said; "with many relatives the process is inverted."

"Do not attend to what Dick says, Mr. Geith," interposed Louisa; "he and Beryl quarrel more when there is nobody by, than they ever do before people."

"That's all you know about it, Solomon," remarked Mr. Elsenham: "Beryl and I have been friends and cronies ever since she wore a short white frock and a sky-blue sash. We robbed birds' nests together, pelted the ducks, laid trains of gunpowder under the cats, chased the fowls, and frightened old women. We quarrelled then. I have a vivid memory of long scratches on my face, for scratching and pulling my hair was Beryl's way of showing fight. We quarrel still; but we were good friends then, and we are good friends now, are we not, coz?"

"Capital at a distance," answered Beryl, who was by this time almost at a white heat.

"And near at hand, too, *ma mignonne*," retorted Mr. Elsenham. "What a heavenly day this is, to be sure. Have you had Zillah out, Matilda?"

"Yes, I had a long ride," answered the beauty; "but I must try for the future to be either earlier or later. The evenings would be the pleasantest time, I think."

"I can assure you they would for me," observed Mr. Elsenham. "Never could see the fun of getting up early in the morning: never could see the beauty of sunrise and dew-drops; and all the rest of the rubbish:" and Mr. Elsenham knocked the ash off his cigar, and waited to hear if any one would contradict him.

No person did, however; George had made up his mind not to argue with Miss Molozane's *fiancé* if he could help it. He saw he was an individual who the more he was contradicted sought all the more occasion for argument; and the accountant was determined to keep his promise and his temper, if he could.

Which forbearance brought its own reward, for Mr. Elsenham took an opportunity of remarking to Miss Molozane that for a tradesman Geith seemed a devilishly decent sort of fellow; appears a confounded deal too much at home with you all, though. Wonder at my uncle allowing it Has he been making love to Beryl?

"Making love to Beryl!" and Miss Molozane opened her fine eyes in astonishment.

"D—— it, you did not think I should imagine he had been making love to you," retorted her betrothed. "I don't see any symptom of softness, remember; but still I thought I'd ask the question."

"How could such an idea enter your head?" asked Miss Molozane. "The man is well enough for his station; but he is only an accountant; he is only here on business."

"He seems to find his business remarkably pleasant," said her cousin, and who could say but that his idea was correct?

"One cannot have a person in the house and not speak a civil sentence to him," observed Miss Molozane.

"Did I say you could; but that is different. Here I find you all gathered together on the terrace, talking, laughing, making yourselves as agreeable as may be, to a man about whom my uncle knows nothing, except that he can add up a column and cast accounts."

"He had been hard at work all day," Matilda explained. "I think Beryl coaxed him out. She never likes to see any one working too much."

"Beryl again!" muttered Mr. Elsenham; "Beryl will get herself into a mess some of these days, if she does not take care."

"I shall begin to think you are in love with

Beryl," said Miss Molozane, with an angry flush. "You seem to think no soul should come to the house but yourself. Last time it was Mr. Werne; now Mr. Geith. Pray, let Beryl manage her own affairs; she is quite competent to keep herself safe without your help. You ought to have more consideration for her than even to mention her name in the same breath with Mr. Geith; who may be a respectable married man for anything we know to the contrary."

"Stuff!" exclaimed Mr. Elsenham. "The fellow is not married. He knows a precious deal too well how to make himself comfortable amongst single women to have any tie at home."

"That may be your opinion," said Miss Molo-zane; "but Beryl has always declared he was either married or a widower."

"Who was either married or widower?" asked Beryl, entering the drawing-room with Louisa at the moment.

"Mr. Geith. Richard says he is sure he is nothing of the kind."

"Shall we ask him, Dick?" inquired Beryl. "Louisa could easily inquire how his wife supported his long absence. Could not you, Louey?"

" Which of you, should I say, wanted to know ?" demanded that young lady.

" You could say we were all dying to become acquainted with Mrs. Geith," suggested Mr. Elsenham ; " and that it would add greatly to the pleasure we are deriving from her husband's society, if she could be induced to come to Withefell with him."

" You might add also, Louey," said Beryl, " that Dick is wearied of our society, and wants something fresh."

" He stops at the ' Stag,' I suppose ?" went on Mr. Elsenham. " You could tell him there is capital accommodation there for families, church close as hand, doctor over the way."

" He does not stop at the ' Stag' at all !" exclaimed Louisa. " He stops here."

" In this house ?" demanded Mr. Elsenham. " Do you mean he eats, drinks, sleeps here ?"

" To be sure he does," answered Louisa. " Where else would you have had him eat, drink, and sleep ?"

" Well, I'll be hanged if ever I heard anything like this !" cried Mr. Elsenham. " My uncle must be stark staring mad. He had better send round the crier and gather in all the tramps in the country. I must speak to him about it."

"If you want to do so," said Beryl, "you'll find him in the library with Mr. Geith."

"Oh ! I am not going to say anything before the man. What, in the name of Heaven, Beryl, do you think I am made of, to imagine I'd insult him in that way ?"

"I had not the slightest idea what Mr. Richard Elsenham's exquisite tact might suggest as the proper course," retorted Beryl, with a curtsy. "But, see ! there is papa in the garden ; you had better go to him and get it over at once."

Taking the hint, Mr. Elsenham walked out to his uncle, and began :

"About Mr. Geith——"

"Well, Richard ?"

"The girls tell me he is staying here at present."

"What then ?"

"Do you think it well, considering his station in life ?"

"Sir !" and Mr. Molozane faced round on his nephew.

"I only meant to say," went on Mr. Elsenham.

"Say nothing," interrupted his uncle ; "that is, say nothing, if you intended for a moment to dictate whom I should, or should not ask into this house. If I like to invite a groom to dinner, it is no business of yours. It is optional with you whether you choose to meet him or not."

" But, considering my engagement to Matilda?" suggested Mr. Elsenham.

" That engagement was none of my seeking," answered his uncle; "and if it had been, it would still give you no right to meddle in my concerns."

"But surely, sir, I may give an opinion concerning the acquaintances of my future wife?"

" You shall not express any opinion to me concerning the acquaintances I introduce to my daughter," thundered Mr. Molozane; " so long as she lives under my roof she shall be civil to my guests; and so long as you come here I shall look for a similar courtesy to them from you."

" I have certainly no intention of being rude to Mr. Geith," answered the young man, meekly; ''And when I spoke I was not thinking so much about Matilda, as about Beryl."

" Which of my daughters is it, Mr. Elsenham, that you are going to do me the honour of marrying?" asked Mr. Molozane. " If it be Matilda, may I request that you will cease troubling yourself in any way about Beryl's prospects? From the curates at Wattisbridge up, you have always fancied every man you have met here wanted to marry Beryl; and once for all, Richard, I tell you I have had enough of this. Do not compel me to express my wishes on this subject again."

" But may I not ask you, sir, whether you know anything about Mr. Geith? About his——"

" That is the way to Wattisbridge," said Mr. Molozane, cutting across his nephew's speech; " and there is the way into my house. If you are going to meddle in my affairs, I must request you to take the former; but if you decide on remaining here, you can only remain on the terms I have mentioned. Mr. Geith is staying in my house as my guest, because it suits us both that he should do so; and unless you intend to treat him as your equal in all respects, it will be well for you to return to London."

" You shall have no reason to complain of any want of civility on my part," said Mr. Elsenham, sullenly. " I like the fellow well enough; I only thought it right to tell you my opinion."

" Having told it to me, you had better let the subject drop," answered Mr. Molozane; and the two went in to dinner.

CHAPTER III.

HAPPINESS.

TAKING it as a whole, Mr. Geith did not find that the new comer interfered, in the slightest degree, with his comfort or convenience. Nay, rather, as the days went by, it seemed as though Mr. Elsenham's presence made the former social freedom greater, and tended to establish the accountant more firmly in his host's favour.

Owing to some curious perversity, Mr. Elsenham took kindly to the man he had wanted to get out of the house. For a couple of evenings he had been cool, not to say sulky; but after that, satisfied perhaps that George neither meant nor was doing any harm, he was graciously pleased to unbend towards him, and evince such courtesy as he could.

If such a thing were possible, there was more life about the Dower House after his arrival than before; what with Beryl and Mr. Elsenham quarrelling, Beryl and Mr. Elsenham disputing, Beryl and Mr. Elsenham laughing, the place was never quiet. From first thing in the morning till all separated for the night, the house was never still. When he left for St. Margaret's, when he returned from town, George heard the same pleasant clatter of tongues; without which he found his London office silent and lonely.

Light-hearted youth! Shall we not bare our heads, and thank God for your cheerful tones, your sunny smiles, your happy carelessness? Shall those who have passed through the heat and burden of weary days, not thank the Almighty for suffering the cool breath of morning to fan their cheeks once more? Shall the old not be grateful for having the burden of years pushed aside for a moment by young and eager hands? Shall they not gaze gladly over the once familiar prospects, even though their eyes be wet with tears; and if, in the young, God be pleased to give them back their own far-away youth for a season, shall they not bask in the sunshine, and listen to the pleasant joy-bells, murmuring the while a trembling thanks-giving?

My readers, pardon me if I linger over this summer-time too lovingly; over those hours which were full of such a delicious sweetness, that George Geith might have been pardoned had he wished to die then, and escape in the midst of his joy from the chance of the dark, and evil days to come.

There are some landscapes from which it is hard to turn our eyes: some lands from which we are loath to turn our feet: some places where we have been so unutterably happy, that they seem to float in the sunbeams for ever after. Like the hills lying under the blue summer sky, like the sea spreading in sunlit glory, like fields and trees bathed in the living beauty of morning, was that time to the man whose youth was past.

Had he ever known youth? he asked himself, as he drank in the wine of that, to him, strange vintage. Had he ever been young, ever been gay, ever been happy, like those people by whom he was surrounded?

Light-hearted youth! the stern, grave man yielded to the charm of your spell; you laid your wand upon him, and behold! the years vanished, and you gave him back the days gone by.

Light-hearted-youth! How shall I chant your praises: by what means can I echo the sound of your glad voices: how may I tell of the smiles, discourse of the laughter; shout to deaf ears the magic influence you possess; persuade those who frown at your gaiety how good a thing it is for us to be near the young, and to join in their mirth?

Shall we put old heads on young shoulders? God forbid! Shall we tell of the night to day, or speak of winter to the spring? Rather, oh friends! shall we not think in the darkness, of the light, in the snow of the sunshine, and retrace our own steps, sooner than drag the young from the happy fields, where they wander among flowers, to the dusty roads and the barren highways along which manhood plods its way.

This was a glad time to George Geith, one in which he lived so fully in the present, that future and past seemed alike indifferent. Such hours as those, bathed in sunshine, steeped in honey, men who have passed their first youth know how to value, because they know, also, how seldom they may return. Holidays may come, summer after

summer, to the schoolboy; but holidays to be
enjoyed are rare in after life. For this reason
manhood gathers all flowers of happiness that
come in its way with such eagerness of pleasure as
can only coexist with pain. It has no spare buds
to fling away, no such profusion of garlands that it
can afford to leave one to wither. The simplest
wild flower is to it as the costliest exotic; and
there are no neglected roses, no drooping lilies, no
withering leaves strewed carelessly along the path
which has been trodden by the feet of middle
age.

I do not know how it is that there are some
middle-aged people who do not care for morning,
or spring, or youth, or happy voices, or ringing
laughter; who regard gaiety as an insult, merriment as a weakness, happiness as a frivolity; who
care for nothing in their daily life but food and
raiment, and dreary dinner-parties, and what they
are pleased to call sensible conversation; who think
there is no wisdom in smiles superior to their own
sedateness; who believe that the Lord Almighty,
who made the flowers to bloom and the trees to
blossom, and the birds to sing, did not intend likewise the young to be gay and happy of necessity,

and the old to be gay and happy likewise, if they found it possible to float with light hearts over the waves of the ocean of life.

George Geith, at any rate, was not one of those who would neither rejoice nor let others do so.

He had suffered, he had worked, he had led a lonely, loveless life; but yet, when these children with whom he was thrown piped unto him, he was ready to dance to their strains.

Happy holidays! Would I had space to linger over those sunlit hours! Spite of the frowns of readers, of the rebukes of critics, I could bask in that summer glory for ever, and chronicle the events of each passing hour with the loving garrulity of age.

Happy holidays!—in which, though it might be the school-children were not all good, all innocent, they were yet all happy and noisy as crickets; when one would have imagined there was no such thing on earth as care, no such shadow as ruin hanging over the Dower House; when it was idleness, jesting, laughing, walking, riding, all the day long; when even George's reluctant labour seemed industry itself, when compared with the labours of those about him.

Never, since he began business, had a summer brought so little work with it to him.

Everybody seemed to be out of town—abroad, at the sea-side, in the Highlands, at Killarney, or the English lakes. Scarcely any books needed balancing; there were no schedules to prepare; but few columns to add up, and accordingly it came to pass that after a time the accountant did not go often into town, but remained much at Withefell, arranging Mr. Molozane's affairs.

How he managed to get those affairs into order, it would be difficult to tell; for it was against the wishes of the whole family that he did any work at all.

" What a pity it seems for you, Mr. Geith, not to be enjoying this lovely weather," Mr. Molozane would say.

" Ah! do come out;" Beryl would plead, laying her hand on his papers, and taking possession of his ink.

" We are going away for a long walk," Mr. Elsenham would observe; " you had better come, too, before your feet grow to the carpet;" whilst Louisa was more peremptory still, and would as coolly take up her position in the library, and announce her intention of giving Mr. Geith " no rest" till he left off work, as if it were in the right and natural course of things for a business man to be tormented to death by a miss in her earliest teens.

"I shall certainly have to lock you out, Miss Loo," George would threaten.

"I should come in through the window," retorted Louisa, from her favourite perch, which was one of the steps of the book-ladder.

"I must then fasten the window," remarked George.

"And draw down the blinds, and close the shutters, and get in candles," suggested Louisa. "Short of that you will not keep me away. I will have you out: you shall not sit here the whole day long, write writing, add adding, till you drop down dead."

"But you write?" said the accountant.

"I write for pleasure; my writing is very different from yours," answered Louisa, with dignity.

"So it may be; but still I am able to make my business my pleasure too."

"Then it is not good for you to have so much pleasure," said the young lady; "and you shall come out into the garden. I cannot imagine what flowers, and fields, and trees, were given people for, if they never look at them."

"Some people look at them, if others do not," George answered; "just as some people see the Pyramids, whilst others never so much as hear of them."

"That is no reason why you should mope in the house all day: do come out: if you don't come fast they will all be gone; for Beryl is going to ride to-day."

"What is she going to ride?" asked George.

"Her own pony. What else should she ride? Perhaps you would like to see her mounted on the top of Dick's Giraffe."

"Indeed I should like to see no such thing," answered the accountant, as he dipped his pen in the ink, and prepared to commence work again.

"Are you not coming after all?" demanded Louisa, descending from her perch, and looking at him as though he had done her some injury.

"I shall come to see them start, if you allow me," he answered; "but I must finish what I am about now."

"You are a monster, and I cannot bear you," said Louisa.

"I have Scripture on my side, at any rate; and I must try to support your displeasure."

"Scripture—what Scripture?" demanded the young lady.

"I shall not tell you," answered George; "but if you can find out for yourself, I will say whether your guess be right."

"But—do—do—do!" pleaded Louisa.

"Surely you would not have me tell untruths? and I said you must guess first," he replied. "And now, Miss Loo, do run away; I cannot get on with a thing whilst you are here."

"But I may come back when I guess."

"If you do not come back too often," he answered; and Louisa left him.

During the next hour she was in about every ten minutes, proving wrong each time; until at last, after a longer absence than usual, he heard through the open window an argument on the terrace outside.

"You shall not."

"I shall."

"I won't be friends with you, Loo."

"Then don't be friends."

"But it is so naughty and unkind of you."

"Naughty, indeed! Who put it into my head? I had forgotten till just now; and I am so glad you reminded me of it."

" I declare, Loo, I shall tell papa."

" Do, and I shall tell papa too; but I shall first ask Mr. Geith. Beryl says, Mr. Geith," she continued, putting her head in at the window, "that your text is, ' Resist the devil, and he will flee from you.' "

"Never mind her, Mr. Geith," put in Beryl; "she is talking nonsense."

"Never mind Beryl, Mr. Geith," said Louisa, "she is telling fibs."

"I shall box your ears, miss," threatened her sister.

"And, Mr. Geith, do come here for a minute," entreated Louise.

"Now, Louey, you might for once do what I ask you," interposed Beryl.

"Dick and Beryl want to know," went on this *enfant terrible*, "how Mrs.———"

"I'll tell you what we said, Mr. Geith," broke in Beryl: "Dick thought you were not married, and I thought you were; and then I remarked that if he liked, Louey might ask which of us was right.

But I never meant her to tell you; and she knew I did not;" and Beryl looked as if she were going to cry about the matter.

"They were arguing again this afternoon," explained Miss Louisa; who, being somewhat curious on the subject herself, was determined to have her say out.

" Dick said 'he'd be ——,' and Louise nodded her head significantly, 'if you were married at all,' and Beryl said she was sure you were, that she had never been mistaken yet: did not you, Beryl?"

But Beryl was gone. Failing to stop her sister's tongue, the next best thing seemed to be to get out of the way of hearing it.

" Dick laid five to one," ran on Miss Louisa, "and Beryl bet a pair of gloves and her riding-whip, to show she was in earnest. So, which wins, Mr. Geith? I am to have a sovereign out of the five if Dick be wrong."

But Mr. Geith would not say which was right. "You would be too wise if you knew everything, Miss Louisa," he observed.

" But I should like so much to know," she urged.

" And I should like so much not to tell you,"

he answered, "that I must hold my peace; besides, it would be such a pity for your sister to lose her whip."

" Then you are not married ?"

" Or for Mr. Elsenham to have to pay five pounds," went on George, coolly.

" They could not both lose, you know," said Louisa.

" Yes, they might," answered the accountant.

" How might they ?"

" If I were divorced," he answered.

" Oh, my goodness gracious !" exclaimed the young lady; " I believe you are."

And she rushed straight off to Mr. Elsenham, with " You've lost, Dick—he's divorced !"

" He's your grandmother !" retorted Mr. Elsenham.

" He is not; I wish he were, instead of the one I have got! But you've lost. Give me my sovereign."

"Who said I had lost ?"

" He said you would both lose if he were divorced."

" Ifs might fly, if they had wings," remarked Mr. Elsenham. " Now, Loo, be off, and tell those sisters of yours to make haste. The horses will be round in five minutes."

" But, about my sovereign, Dick ?"

" Earn it, young lady," was Mr. Elsenham's advice; and he forthwith lit a cigar and walked away, smoking, as usual, down the avenue.

By the time the ladies were ready, George came round to the lawn to see them start.

" Trot is not much of a steed, is he ?" asked Beryl, patting her pony's neck, a civility which Trot returned by taking her habit in his mouth and making believe to chew it. " I am always miles behind everybody."

" Because you ride so slowly," said her cousin.

" Because you ride so fast," said Beryl.

" What a deal of good a gallop would do you, Geith !" remarked Mr. Elsenham. " What a pity you do not ride !"

George could not help smiling at the observation; and it was such a strange smile in which he indulged, as he stooped and pretended to be adjusting Trot's bridle, that Miss Molozane said:

" Perhaps Mr. Geith does ride. I believe none of us have ever asked him."

" Faith ! perhaps he does, though it's not much

of a City accomplishment. Do you ride?" And Mr. Elsenham turned, with his foot in the stirrup, to ask the question.

" Yes, I have ridden," answered the accountant.

" Any brute like that ?" inquired Mr. Elsenham, pointing to the Giraffe, which it was about to be the groom's privilege to mount.

" No, not much like that ; for an uglier animal I never saw."

" He is a rare fellow to go, for all that. Should you be afraid to venture your neck on him ?"

" Not in the least."

" If you are sure of that, come with us. Take care how you get up. He's a devil to kick."

" Let him kick," was Mr. Geith's philosophic answer.

" Have you ridden in the circus, old fellow ?" asked Mr. Elsenham, when he saw the accountant fairly settled in his saddle.

"I have ridden across country, which I suppose is something the same thing," retorted Mr. Geith.

" After the hounds ?"

" Do people generally go across the country before them ?" inquired George.

"Hang it, no. I meant, have you been in the habit of hunting?"

"I was, years ago."

"Where? In the neighbourhood of London?"

"No; in Bedfordshire."

"Is that your county?"

"It is not the county where I was born; but it is the county where most of the Geiths have lived."

"You don't mean that you are one of the Geiths of Snareham?"

"Would there be anything wonderful if I did?"

"Are you any relation to Sir Mark Geith?"

"Only his cousin."

"Good Lord!" ejaculated Mr. Richard Elsenham. "How does it happen that you are an accountant?"

"If I were inclined to be polite, I might ask how it happens you are a gentleman at large," asked Mr. Geith, with a slight sneer.

"You deserved that, Dick," said Beryl. "What affair is it of yours what Mr. Geith chooses to be?"

"It is, perhaps, not my choice, but my necessity, Miss Beryl," observed George, reining in his horse beside her; to which the young lady replied in a

low tone, something about her cousin being always
inquisitive and impertinent.

"I shall come to you, Beryl, when I want a
thoroughly good character," said Mr. Elsenham,
who caught some part of her sentence. "If I have
offended Mr. Geith, I am sorry for it. Would you
wish me to say anything more than that?"

"There was no reason why you should have said
so much," answered George, laughing. "I am not
ashamed of being connected with the Geiths of
Snareham; and I am still less ashamed of being
an accountant in the City."

Whereupon Mr. Elsenham was so good as to
assure their new companion that he meant for the
future to forget all about the City, and his business
too.

"But I cannot agree to that, Mr. Elsenham,"
answered the accountant. The City has given me
a home; my business has provided bread and
cheese; and I am not going to follow the example
of the citizens, and despise that which has kept
me off the parish. Business is a capital invention,
and the City is a place where any man with courage
and industry may push his way. The City is
the proper land for younger sons to emigrate

to, if younger sons could but be induced to think so."

"Bravo, Mr. Geith," said Beryl, clapping her hands; which demonstration caused the Giraffe to plunge frantically: and induced Mr. Elsenham to remark they had better get on a little faster, and breathe the horses before they became troublesome.

CHAPTER IV.

BERYL'S ADMIRER.

IT was not long before Beryl's pony fell far behind the rest; so far, indeed, that whenever Mr. Geith could pull in his horse, he turned and rode back some distance to meet her.

"Never mind me," said Beryl; "go on with the others, and I will overtake you when you commence walking."

"As if it were probable I should leave you," answered George; and the pair rode on in silence for a minute or two.

Then, "I like," began Beryl, "to hear a man stand up for his business, as much as I like to hear people stand up for their country. I think if I had to earn my bread, I should feel the dignity of labour so strongly that I should quarrel with any one who disputed it. We have some neighbours who talk about the City as if it were a den of thieves; and who, although every sixpence they have was made in trade, "could not think of putting their sons to business." They were happy to have had fathers who were not ashamed of trade. But for that, they would now be poor enough."

"They merely express, however, the general prejudice of society," remarked George.

"Do you not think they create that prejudice for themselves?" she asked. "The outer world can know nothing of business, except what it hears from the initiated; and if the initiated declare it is all roguery and vulgarity from chapter to chapter, what is society to say? Remember, Mr. Geith, I believe in business, and I only wish I were a man, to show what business could do for Molozane Park. I have thought a great deal about business lately, and I see that if trade were not always providing money for the aristocracy, the aristocracy would soon go down to the lowest depths of poverty. Look at the Park, Mr. Geith: if we were there now, we could do nothing for want of money; but as it is, Mr. Werne keeps up a fine establishment; gives plenty of employment; is good to the poor;

F 2

is hospitable to his neighbours. I am sure," went on the poor little girl, with a tremor in her voice, "it was a good day for Withefell when the Molozanes left the Park, for we were not rich enough to do anything for any one—not even for ourselves."

"Mr. Werne, then, is very rich?" asked George.

"Nobody knows how rich," answered Beryl, with a sad look in her brown eyes as she spoke. "He is a chemist, and has made—oh! such a fortune! His father was a chemist also, but he never got on like his son. He could buy the Park tomorrow, papa says, and never miss the purchase-money."

"And he is as good as he is rich?" suggested George.

"I could not tell you, Mr. Geith, how good a man he is," said Beryl, earnestly. "Dick laughs at me for praising him, but I cannot help saying what I think—that he is better than any one I ever knew. I do not know how it happens that you have never met him, for he comes often to see papa. That is the principal entrance to the Park," she added; you have not seen it before, and I declare there is Mr. Werne himself!"

Beryl was right : there was Mr. Werne. Mounted on a strong, iron-grey horse, he was coming slowly down the long avenue bordered with elms ; but at sight of Beryl and her companion he quickened his pace.

" We will wait for him," said Beryl, with the utmost composure ; and what could her companion do but follow suit ?—nothing loth, to say truth, for he was curious to see Mr. Werne, and he had now a capital opportunity of doing so.

A light-haired, fair-complexioned, grey-eyed, middle-aged man, to whom Beryl was, George Geith saw at a glance, sun, moon, stars, and planets ; whilst, as for Beryl herself, the accountant might as soon have tried to understand the sphinx as the face of the young lady by his side.

Did she care for this millionaire, or not ? Would she marry for an establishment ? Did she understand what all that devotion of manner, all that repressed eagerness meant ? George began to ask himself these and fifty other similar questions almost before the first greetings were over—before he himself had been introduced to Beryl's friend.

Was the little lady, when all was said and done, hankering, like other people, after loaves and

fishes? after the flesh-pots of Egypt? after the
gold, and the station, and the influence which
confer advantages not to be despised? That she
cared for Mr. Werne, George did not credit; but he
was commencing almost to believe that Beryl was
not blind to her own interests; and he thought, for
a moment, that perhaps she was exalting this man
into a god, so as afterwards to excuse her own
worship of him. Poor Beryl! the day came when
this old, uncharitable man of the world knew her
better; but that day was not the one on which he
rode along the Hertfordshire lanes, listening to all
Mr. Werne had to say to her.

Very much in the way Mr. Geith felt, and he
wished in his heart that one of the trio was
absent—either himself or Mr. Werne; but as it
was, so it was; and he heard the decorous talk
about the poor and their wants, their sickness, their
improvidence, their necessities, which had been so
familiar to him once, in the days when he was
professing to serve another God, than Mammon.

In the one time, as at the other, George found
the talk detestable. There are three topics which,
to a man of his nature, must always, I suspect,
prove wearisome, viz., servants, children, and the

poor. He never could understand the interest people took in any of them ; and for the moment he felt inclined to hold with Mr. Elsenham, that the Withefell saint was an awful humbug, and a tremendous bore.

Beryl's propriety likewise was something dreadful to contemplate. Not once, but fifty times, George had heard her making fun of the very men and women in whose behalf she was now so eloquent.

She had been good enough to imitate old Mrs. Mears' whine, Job Darth's stammer, Mrs. O'Rourke's brogue, and Mary Hurst's sniffle. She had gone over every soul in the village, *seriatim*, mocking their peculiarities, hitting off their characteristics, baring their falseness, and yet still here she was, riding along with as demure a face as though she had never ridiculed any living being.

"And about Beames' rent, Mr. Werne? I believe he is now in constant work?"

"I can't stand this any longer," thought George, and thought it with the addition of an oath; and while Mr. Werne was answering, he struck his horse stealthily yet sharply, causing him to dance and curvet across the road.

"You have not a very quiet animal, sir," observed

Mr. Werne; in answer to which Mr. Geith muttered some almost inaudible reply, whilst he struck the horse again, reining him in tightly as he did so.

Straight up went the brute on his hind legs, and forthwith Beryl became. alarmed, and cried out :

"You will be killed ! pray don't strike him ; you don't know what horrid tempers all Dick's horses have."

" I know this is rather an awkward animal to manage at a walk," answered George, not without a certain satisfaction ; whilst Mr. Werne said, courteously, he thought in the stables at the Park he might surely find something to suit him better, and that he hoped he would come and take his choice.

Just then Mr. Elsenham and Miss Molozane appeared in sight. " They had come back," they said, "to see if Beryl and Mr. Geith were safe;" and they shook hands with Mr. Werne, and remarked on the heat of the weather, and the beauty of the day, with most praiseworthy politeness.

By-and-by, Mr. Elsenham and George dropped behind, Mr. Werne escorting the ladies in front.

" So you have been favoured with a sight at

last," remarked the younger man, when they were out of earshot. " What do you think of Beryl's saint ?"

"That he is like all other saints," was the reply.

" In what respect ?"

" Too meek—too good—too much like an old woman," said George, as he touched his horse with his whip again.

"Now I tell you what, my good fellow," cried Mr. Elsenham, " if you try that, you'll come to grief to a certainty ; Giraffe won't stand it."

" Giraffe must stand it," was the reply.

"But he rears."

" I know he does ; he was rearing a few minutes since."

" And why can't you let him alone ?"

" Because I am sick of being quiet ; because I am tired to death of this pace ; because I hate talk about the poor."

" Hear, hear !" said Mr. Elsenham, approvingly.

" Why, in Heaven's name," went on the accountant, " can't they get their wine and their jelly, and their physic and their clothing, and their alms, without such an everlasting clatter about their wants ? I'm sure I should think it trouble enough to see to their necessities, without having to talk them over afterwards."

"D—— the poor!" said Mr. Elsenham with great gusto. "But, after all, the poor are sometimes only made a pretext, as in the present case. Over tracts, flannel petticoats, and beef tea, Beryl and Mr. Werne carry on their courtship. If ever she marries that Pope, she and I are quits, for there will be no fun, and no life in her afterwards."

"Miss Beryl might do worse, nevertheless," remarked George, sententiously.

"That's the deuce of the matter. If the man were poor, one might find something to say; but as it is, so it is."

"Gold wins the day all the world over," remarked the accountant; and he thought of the man beside him whom Matilda was going to marry, and of the man riding in front with whom Beryl was coquetting.

For what else could he call it? If she liked him, why did she not encourage him? If she did not like him, why did she praise him up to the skies, and listen to him so demurely?

He was trying to solve what we have all tried

vainly to solve sometime or another, the enigma of
a neighbour's heart. He was judging of its works
from the way he saw the hands moving. He
thought he knew all the wheels within wheels that
were spinning round in the girl's mind, and accordingly, because he would not acknowledge that man
knows nothing of man, he judged, as we all judge
when we condemn others besides ourselves, wrongly.

In the midst of our sin, in the midst of our folly,
in the midst of our weakness, there is one consolation of which the preacher never tells us, namely,
that it is not with man, but with God, the last
sentence rests. How would it fare with us if our
neighbour had to dispose of our souls? if he had
to tell our motives, recount our deeds? I think
about this when I hear man's verdict—man's
righteous verdict according to man's light—on the
thief and the murderer. I think that another
volume which is to us a sealed book has been read
up on high, and that the other side, over which, it
may be, angels' tears have fallen, has been pleaded
before that only tribunal where all man's misery,
his temptations, his antecedents, his weaknesses,
his terror, his blindness, his feeble strivings after
light, are fully understood.

Is this talk about a girl and her lover too grave?
I believe not. There is not a relation of life in
which we are not given to judging over-righteously.

There is nothing which offends humanity so
much as the loneliness of its fellow human being.
Though we lock our own doors, dry our own tears,
smile our forced smiles, talk our lightest words
when our fellows come near to probe the wounds we
would cover away from sight, we are still angry and
offended because they will not tell us of their
ailments, because the cry of mortality in its
bitterest anguish is ever, "Leave me with my
God"—its most earnest prayer to its eager fellows
to be left alone—alone!

I think it must be greatly for this cause that we
like the young; because, even though the pages of
their book be blank, we are permitted to look over
them; and it might be for the same reason, viz.,
because she was young, that George Geith, who
had his secret coffined and buried, was angry with
Beryl for being what he called double-faced; for
having her little by-play, too.

Practical man as he was, he never paused to ask
himself what all this interest meant; what all this
jealousy indicated; but talked on in his anger,

while shallow Dick Elsenham read him through and through, and thought, with a half-compassionate contempt, that it would be rather good fun if the one business man tried to cut out the other. He knew, or thought he knew, George would have no chance with either father or daughter; though, to be sure, the Snareham connection put a new aspect on affairs. He might as well inquire a little further into that.

"I forget what relation you said you were to Sir Mark Geith," he said, as they rode still behind the others.

"Cousin," was the reply. "His father and mine were brothers."

"Then you are the next heir, I suppose?"

"Not I! There is a certain uncle; there are probable children; there are twenty other things between me and Snareham."

"Sir Mark is not married, though."

"Is he not? He and his wife, at any rate, were at my office not a month since," said George, almost rejoicingly. "You seem to take a wonderful interest in my relations, Mr. Elsenham," he added. "May I inquire if you know any of them?"

"I have met your cousin," answered the other, slowly. "I have met him where I think he was making his money spin. He plays infernally high, Mr. Geith."

"I suppose he has a right to do what he likes with his own," answered George.

"You do not appear particularly to care about him or his doings," remarked Mr. Elsenham.

"I care enough," was the reply; "but what would you have? Mark's way and mine lie in opposite directions. I cannot leave my path to follow his; and if I could, I am not aware that he would thank me for my pains. There is too wide a distinction between us for there to be much sympathy."

"Do you know much of him?" asked Mr. Elsenham.

"Had we been brothers I could scarcely at one time have known more," was the reply; "but there comes a day, as you are aware, when the rich and the poor must separate; and that day came long ago to us. He turned to his pleasure, I to my business; and every year as it passes by must separate us more and more."

"He was a good-hearted fellow, I think?" said Mr. Elsenham.

" Never a better breathed," answered George.

"Could he not have got you some appointment?" asked Mr. Elsenham.

" My dear sir," said George, with a look of the most profound compassion, " I do not want an appointment. I hang on my own hook, which I find a great deal stronger than any hook could be, that was put up for me by another man."

" But the social standing?" suggested Mr. Elsenham.

" Social standing is success," answered the accountant, with a smile. " The incarnation of social success is riding before us. When I am rich enough to live in a place like Molozane Park, I shall have secured my standing likewise."

" What are you two talking about?" asked Miss Molozane, turning at the moment to speak to the pair, who had gradually been drawing nearer and nearer to their companions.

"About the poor; about the rich; about business; about the City," replied her cousin.

" Somewhat unusual subjects for you to discuss, are they not?" inquired Mr. Werne.

" I believe so," was the answer; " but getting into good company makes even fools wise for the time being ; and Mr. Geith's conversation is of so practical a character, that I cannot choose but follow suit."

" Mr. Geith affects the City a little, I think I have understood," remarked Mr. Werne.

" Mr. Geith affects that which butters his bread," replied the accountant ; " no more, no less. Though it is but a modicum which has been allowed me, I am still thankful not to have to eat my morsel dry."

" A sensible man to be a younger son, is he not, Mr. Werne ?" demanded Mr. Elsenham, stroking his moustache. " If work were not such a confounded bore, he would almost persuade me to visit your El Dorado, and see whether I, too, could not work a gold mine. It is a great thing to be earnest in anything, is it not? See how soon he has made a disciple of me."

Doubtfully Mr. Werne looked from the one man to the other before he said :

" I did not think it had been possible to convert Mr. Elsenham ; and I congratulate you, Mr. Geith, on your success."

" Mr. Geith has the true missionary gift," remarked the younger man. " He knows how to stroke his cats without turning their hair the wrong way. Ah! if missionaries could only comprehend the way of the grain, what a number of pussies they might have purring after them!"

"Pussies have claws; so your simile is unfortunate, Dick," said Beryl.

"But, with judicious management, claws may be cut, Miss Beryl," suggested George, who took pleasure at the moment in following his companion's lead. "I must, however," he added, "disclaim, Mr. Werne's implied compliment on my success, for I have achieved none. It merely so happened that Mr. Elsenham and I agreed on a few points, and went together into them."

"You and Dick agreed!" said Beryl, with a look of astonishment. "On what points, may I ask?"

"It is not good for little girls to know too much," answered her cousin; "and, besides, I want to inquire if we are to get home to-day; because, if we are, I think we had better alter our pace."

"My road lies to Withefell Hall," said Mr. Werne, "so I will not detain you longer;" and he forthwith shook hands with the ladies; and touching his hat to the gentlemen, before raising it in final salute to the party, turned out of the sunshine to let them pass.

"A good riddance," observed Mr. Elsenham, who was striving with all his might to accommodate his horse's long trot to the awful little canter of Beryl's pony: "when Mr. Werne takes up his parable, I always long to send him a gown and bands."

"And when I hear you talking against him, I always long to ornament you with a pair of donkey's ears," said Beryl, pettishly.

"Mr. Geith was so charmed with his conversation," went on the young man; "he likes the poor so much, and thinks stories of their thrift, and providence, and necessity, so interesting and so instructive. The contrast, likewise, between Beryl a sinner and Beryl a saint was delicious. Why are you not a saint at home, cousin? You have no idea how much nicer we should all think you."

"I won't ride with you any more: I won't speak to you. I hate you, Dick," said Beryl, and she pulled up her pony short.

"Not you," answered her cousin, taking Trot's rein, and pulling him into a gallop; "you like me a precious sight better than you like Mr. Werne, when all is said and done."

"I do not; I can't bear you; and I never could;

and you shan't pull my pony; and I will go home
by myself."

"Would it go home by itself? and would it tell
its papa that bad people teazed it when it was a
saint? and said it had two faces, one for a wicked
world, and one for the immaculate owner of Molozane Park? and would it cry, and look pitiful?
Will it dry its eyes on Trot's mane? or shall I go
after Mr. Werne to perform that operation for it?"

"I'll tell you what I shall do when I get home,"
said Beryl; "box your ears soundly."

"If it would improve your temper, box them
now;" and Mr. Elsenham stooped down his head
to receive the threatened punishment; but Beryl
would not be appeased. She rode steadily on;
both hands on her reins, looking straight ahead,
till she suddenly turned to George and said:

"And you are just as bad as Dick. I thought
better of you, Mr. Geith, I did."

"Now, it is your turn," remarked Mr. Elsenham,
"give it to him well, Beryl; you don't know half
he said against your idol."

"I said, Miss Beryl, that which I am prepared
to stand to," observed George, who was never slow
to take up the cudgels in his own behalf. "I

never could see, and I never shall see, the good of
talking so much about the poor : I was not particularly impressed with Mr. Werne—nor at all
interested in his conversation; but, at the same
time, I do not doubt his being a most excellent
man; and am willing to admit that my want of
appreciation may arise from a want of taste."

"He wearies me," said Matilda; "how Beryl
can listen to him as she does, is a complete puzzle.
For my part, I think he has completely destroyed
the pleasure of our ride."

"You needn't have come back to ride with him,"
pouted Beryl.

"We will remember your hint next time," said
Mr. Elsenham; but Beryl would not answer, nor
take any notice of him. She was looking with
such a reproachful expression at the accountant
that his heart melted towards her, and he felt
bound to do battle in her behalf.

"If I recant, may I be forgiven, Miss Beryl?"
he asked, in a low tone; and the result was what
might have made many another swear black to be
white; for she pulled her pony away from Dick,
and riding round to the other side of Mr. Geith,
took refuge between the hedge and Giraffe.

" I am very sorry to have offended you," he said.

" It was not your fault; you do not know Mr. Werne as I know him. When you do, you will think differently."

"I am ready to think differently now, if you desire it," remarked Mr. Geith; whereupon Mr. Elsenham laughed, and declared the accountant was as great a humbug as Mr. Werne—a compliment which that gentleman received with perfect temper.

" If I were only as good," he began.

" It would be well for you," finished Beryl, snappishly; and the short-lived truce was broken.

CHAPTER V.

BERYL EXPLAINS.

THERE was one comfort with Beryl Molozane,
that, if she had little fits of ill humour, she did not
stay long in them; and if she had periods of
gravity and propriety, they were short in comparison with the long summer days, which she could
fill with laughter and glee.

Always after she had got up on a pedestal and
made a saint of herself, Beryl was sure to plunge
into deeper depths than ever of fun and mockery.
If she could once be got to laugh, all her solemnity
vanished, and the house rang again with the sound
of her mirth.

And a dull house it would have been without
Beryl, as George Geith, sitting over his papers,
acknowledged. She was to that place what the

breath of life is to the body: the moving power, the animating cause, which kept the blood flowing through the veins, and smiles brightening the face. Her voice seemed never silent; her tongue never still. From the garden her gay tones came into the room where the accountant sate at work; lingering amongst the roses he found her when it grew too dark for him to see to do more.

"We are going to have a visitation on Monday, Mr. Geith," she said. "Granny is coming—Granny and her train."

"Her train?" repeated George, who was a little mystified.

"Yes; Granny, like other great ladies, cannot travel without one; and she would bring more people, only that papa won't have them here. As it is, she has her maid and Mr. Elsenham—old Mr. Elsenham I mean, her brother-in-law—and old Mr. Elsenham's man; and she comes in a great chariot, which puts up at the "Stag," at Wattisbridge, in company with her coachman and two footmen. She brought her butler down the last time, but I do not think she will try that again. He had a great deal to say to our cook about there being no servants' hall, and at last came

to me, to observe he had not been accustomed
to it."

"Did he tell you to what he had been accustomed?" asked her companion.

"No; I did not ask him, or probably he would;
but I told him I was very sorry, and that if he had
any suggestions to make as to what he would like,
I should be glad to hear it. The beauty of it was,"
went on Beryl, "he knew I was making fun of
him, though he could not find a word to say,
except that ' No; he had no suggestion to make.'
Then, said I, I do not see what I can do, for I
am afraid grandmamma might not like me to
have you in the drawing-room; but if you choose,
I will ask her."

"What did he say then?" inquired Mr. Geith.

"He did not say anything to me," answered
Beryl, "but he went straight off to Granny, and
gave her notice; and she actually raised his wages
and prayed him to stop; and he was graciously
pleased to consent, only papa said he should not
stop here; and so she had to send him back to
London, and I wish they would all stay there."

"Why does she not come by the Eastern Counties line?" asked George, with a natural wonder

that any one who could help it should put herself to so much trouble.

"For three reasons. One, she dislikes all railways; another, she cannot get to the Shoreditch station without crossing the City; and a third, she thinks she creates a sensation by coming down with as great a clatter as the Lord Mayor. The people about here think she is mad; that is all she gets in the way of public opinion out of her four horses."

"You don't mean to say that she travels with four horses?" said Mr. Geith.

"She would travel with eight if she could manage it," answered Beryl; "Granny is essentially—but you will see what she is for yourself when you see her. Meantime, I am so glad you are going to stay here to-morrow, so that we may have one day of peace before she comes."

George was glad too; and the intimacy between himself and the family at the Dower House had by this time become so close, that he never thought of uttering those courteous expressions of pleasure, regret, and so forth, which do good duty at the commencement of an acquaintance, but which seem such trumpery coin when acquaintance has ripened into something more, that friend never thinks of offering it to friend.

Accordingly, George Geith did not say he was glad—why, indeed, should he, when he knew that Beryl was perfectly well aware he was pleased to stop?

Thinking of his lonely Sundays in town, thinking of his lonely evenings in Fen Court, thinking of the days when he had not a soul to speak to whom he liked, nor a house at which he cared to visit where he was sure of a welcome, the accountant sometimes became almost unmanned, and wondered how he should be able to endure the old desolate life when he had to return to it in earnest once again.

It is not sorrow, nor toil, nor anxiety, nor difficulty, which tries the strength and endurance of a man like George Geith; but rather joy and happiness. All the world over, natures like his prove the truth of the old fable, in which it was not the strong north wind that beat down the traveller, but rather the beams of a genial sun.

Man bears that trouble to which he is born better than the glad sunshine for which he had no right to look; and it had come by this time to such a pass with George Geith, that, living in the light, he dared not look forth at the darkness into which, sooner or later, he knew he must plunge.

And those Sundays at the Dower House were so pleasant! when he could take his rest without any twinges of conscience about work neglected and hours wasted; when he could loiter over his dressing, listening to the insane co-cooing of the pigeons and the prating of the hens; when he did not consider it his duty to hurry over his breakfast, but could enjoy to the full that sunny morning room, which always in after years came back to his memory with open windows and floating muslin curtains; when the talk was so pleasant, the air so balmy, the place and the people so like home!

Then the leisurely walk across the fields to Wattisbridge! the short, smooth grass on which the ladies' cool muslin dresses made a rustle as of the light wings of birds, the delicious country air, the pleasant country sights, the dancing of the squirrels in the wood, the loveliness of the wild flowers in the hedges, the blue sky, the green earth, and the calm stillness of the Christian Sabbath pervading all things, and underlying, like a soft key-note, the whole music of animated nature!

And what if the pleasure were sensational?
Happy is the man, I think, who can take a sinless
joy out of his senses! to whom Nature does not
exhibit her landscapes, chant her melodies, unveil
her loveliness, all in vain! whom the lights and
sounds and flowers of the summer thrill with a
strange delight, and who can thank God for living
and moving and having his being with the unques-
tioning simplicity of a child!

George Geith never felt so thankful about having resigned his profession as when he came out of
church with Beryl Molozane. Whilst he was a
curate, living within a sacred pale, fenced off to a
certain extent from free contact with the laity, he
never heard how the laity pull their clerical guides
to pieces. With a sudden shock and horror it came
upon him that perhaps in his day he had been
derided and scoffed at too—his manner mimicked,
his tone ridiculed, his mistakes pounced on, his
sermons criticized. It was not healthy, he felt, for
the congregation to be setting itself up in judg-
ment; and yet, if the teachers were like the Wattisbridge clergy—muffs—what then?

He could not contradict the truth of what the
Molozanes said about rectors and curates alike;

but, at the same time, it was not pleasant for a man who had been a clergyman to feel, that instead of himself and his brothers being as he once fondly imagined, teachers, they were rather set up as targets at which all the small witticisms, all the trifling jests of their hearers might be directed.

And had he dared to remind Beryl of the message these Wattisbridge curates brought, he knew she would at once have answered that it was at the messengers, not the message, she was laughing. But he did not dare. George, who in most respects had not been wont to feel cowardly, was now so anxious to keep on good terms with his host's family, that he often held his tongue when he knew he ought to have opened his lips, and when, but for some strange feeling which held him back, he would have liked to speak to her about this mockery of all things (except Mr. Werne), holy and pure, which offended him.

For though he had thrown aside the gown, all *esprit de corps* had not departed also, and he often felt inclined to stand up and do battle for these men, against whom Dick Elsenham and Beryl Molazane were perpetually bending their bows and twanging their arrows.

Capping verses was nothing in comparison to the way this pair amused themselves, capping the peculiarities of the preacher. From the great family pew, which Mr. Molozane had not relinquished with the Park, the two took mental notes, which they compared when they came out of church; and George had heard Beryl, robed in a black silk cloak, with a red shawl hung on behind, delivering a sermon à la Wattisbridge to perfection. He knew when he was listening to her he ought to have gone out of the room, or offered some serious remonstrance, but he had only joined in Dick's laughter, and encouraged Beryl to further literary efforts; not a thing escaped her, not a movement, not a look, and to people who were inclined to laugh Wattisbridge Church offered temptations innumerable.

Often George caught himself thinking, "If I were there, how differently I would have the service performed;" and then he felt devoutly thankful he was not there, and that he never should have to preach again. For had his life depended on it, he knew he could not, after hearing Beryl's comments, be ever able to lift his mind above them, and he began to perceive how fine a thing it is for clergymen, that, though they sometimes hear fault-finding, they never hear ridicule.

What made Mr. Geith more indignant against Beryl, if indignant be not far too strong a word, was, that he knew perfectly well if Mr. Werne were of the party, her tone would have been very different.

As it was, she chattered on—mocking, grimacing, ridiculing—till one might have thought life a puppet show, containing no definite aim in time, no hope for eternity.

George did not like it. He would have been better content to see Beryl down almost in the depths of despair, than to notice that nothing in heaven above, or in the earth beneath, seemed able to make any serious impression upon her. Could she be sorry for long? Could she grieve sincerely? Would it be possible for her to weep without the sunshine breaking through? Was there any earnestness about her? Had she really a heart? In very truth, did she possess a soul? Had women souls at all? he caught himself wondering, when Beryl woke him out of his brown study with—

"Well, Mr. Geith, what treason are you plotting now?"

"I was wondering whether it would be possible

for any man to preach a sermon at which you would not care to laugh."

"I think it would—will you try? We shall have plenty of leisure this afternoon, and we will listen to you as long as you like to talk. You shall take for your text, 'Thou speakest as one of the foolish women speaketh,' if you choose, and none of us will be offended."

"And then you will make fun of me to your heart's content."

"Oh! fie, Mr. Geith; do I make fun of my friends? Can I see anything in them of which to make fun? I suppose you are beginning to think, with Granny, that I can be serious about nothing— that I can feel no trouble—carry no burden."

"If I did think so, should I be wrong, Miss Beryl?" he inquired.

"*Et tu Brute!*" was all the answer he could get out of her; but the brown eyes proved more eloquent than her tongue, and looked reproaches at him—such reproaches, that George felt himself constrained to say:

"The truth is, I have never seen you grave but once, until yesterday; and yesterday——"

"You thought I was not grave in earnest," she

quickly added, as he paused; "and there you were wrong. You imagine, because it is necessary to my existence to laugh at people's oddities, that I never feel for their woes. You think, because I have a quick sense of the ludicrous, that I have no eyes for grief. And there you do me an injustice. You often are unjust to me, Mr. Geith."

" Am I ?" he said ; " tell me how, and I will strive to think all you wish for the future."

" Why, you have got that stupid notion which so many people take up, that the same person cannot be sorry and merry. You fancy that, because I think the poor funny, I do not also think they are often in great distress. They may be humbugs— many of them are —and I see they are humbugs ; but I know, at the same time, that no matter what they may be, they feel heat, and cold, and the want of blankets, and the dearness of coals, and their inability to get meat, just as much as you or I. For this reason, I do my best to get them helped ; but I reserve to myself the privilege of laughing, to prove I am not imposed on ; that I see only their necessities as they are, and not their necessities as they present them for public inspection. Hunger and thirst, Mr. Geith, and the want of fire and clothing, are realities, concerning which I suppose even I may speak gravely if I please."

"Assuredly," answered her companion; "but there are other people besides the poor at whom you laugh; about whom you never speak a grave sentence."

"You are thinking of the unhappy Mr. Grey," she said, laughing. "I must make fun of Mr. Grey, and his light wavy hair; he is so terribly proper; so intensely decorous; one sentence lasts him as long as half a dozen would anybody else; one idea becomes in his hands a volume, sufficient for a whole day's slow conversation.

"But I believe he is an excellent young man," said Mr. Geith, rebukingly.

"Did you ever know any one who was a frightful bore; who could do nothing at a party but sit like a Pope on a hard chair, that was not an excellent young man? I never did, and I have had a large experience of curates: besides, what do I say against Mr. Grey? nothing, except that if he stopped with his text his sermons would be long enough; and that we are not to stare, because his 'mamma,' as he calls her, said he was shy, and that it was not good for him. All that does not prevent my thinking there is something very touching in the way his mother listens to him preaching; and I would not for any consideration let her hear me laughing at him; or say to her that I do not think him a second St. Paul. Indeed, it is quite true that I never look at Mr. Grey without thinking ' He was the only son of his mother, and she was a widow.' "

This was the way Beryl spoiled every sentence she uttered. She never could sketch a grave face, without putting a mocking one behind it. Whether from habit, or from some mental distortion, it seemed impossible for her to disassociate even the most earnest things from the grotesque. The most serious subject had its laughable side; over graves the clown seemed dancing; behind tears there was an imp gibing and grinning.

There seemed nothing earnest in her, save that which is the common heritage of true-hearted women—love. She did not make fun of those she loved. Was that the reason she was grave with Mr. Werne?

George marvelled, and thought he would beat that cover, too.

"How does it happen," he asked, smiling, "that

you never laugh at these things and people when you are with Mr. Werne?"

"How do you know I do not?" she quickly retorted.

"Because your cousin told me so," he answered.

"I shan't tell you—I can't tell you," she almost cried; but then, calming down in a moment, she went on: "Mr. Werne is different from most people. There is a gravity about him which infects even me; he is so earnest himself; he thinks life such a frightfully solemn affair that he makes me solemn in spite of myself. He compels me to feel good and miserable while I am with him. I am not laughing now, Mr. Geith. I am only telling you the honest, sober truth."

And her face changed so while she was speaking that George could not doubt her word; could not think for a moment she was deluding herself, and misleading him; only he wondered more and more as to what it was Beryl really intended, as to what she really meant.

Two minutes after no one would have thought she meant anything; jesting with Mr. Elsenham; laughing at her sister; who could have told what with her was real—what assumed!

Which was the actual nature? that which skimmed through existence on the wings of mirth, or that which looked at life for an instant through tears?

Who may judge? Which of us, friends, may even guess at the true part of our neighbour's nature, when we are incompetent to lay our finger on the sterling metal in our own?

CHAPTER VI.

ACROSS THE FIELDS.

THERE was no evening service at Wattisbridge, and
as it did not suit the Molozanes to attend church
in the afternoon, the three young ladies, their
cousin, and Mr. Geith, walked over in the evening
to Withefell Bottom, a little hamlet lying two
miles on the other side of Withefell proper, where
the vicar held forth on the saving nature of faith,
and buried works out of sight, under a mausoleum
of his own erection.

Beryl was kind enough to give an epitome of
the probable sermon to the quartet after dinner;
and Mr. Geith, who had in clerical days been a
little "high," forbore to blame her, even in his
heart, for her mimicry. Rather he enjoyed the
ridicule; for Mr. Elsenham informed him, privately,

that the vicar was a pet of the Withefell saint;
and that not only the Withefell saint, but the
proprietor of Withefell Hall affected the teaching of
the clergyman who preached faith without works.

" Filthy rags of our own self-righteousness," said
Beryl. " I always fancy bits of red cotton floating
from gooseberry bushes when I hear that; but perhaps Mr. Geith may like the vicar. He is greatly
run after by people who really think all they can
do mere mites in the treasury; and also by those
who would like to go to heaven without working at
all: *vide* Mr. Finch. Eh, Dick ?"

"Mr. Finch be hanged," said Mr. Elsenham in
answer.

" You would have said something else if Mr.
Geith had not been here," observed Louisa.

" It is all the same to me what he is," remarked
her cousin.

" I were the architeck of my own fortunes, I
were," said Beryl, coming down from her pulpit in
a minute. "I never owed no man nothing in the
way of gratitude. I wasn't like you, Mr. Elsenham: you was brought up in the lap of luxury;
you had but to ring for this and t'other, and say,
'John, bring me this; John, fetch me that.' With

me it were, ' Ned, you young beggar, where are you
skulking ?' or ' Ned, you lazy scoundrel, look sharp.'
You loll in carriages, young man. You never rode
in a wan, I'll be bound. I were glad, I were, to
get a post as dog in a wan; I liked that better
nor ever I did since I made my fortune, riding in
a carridge like a swell. Well, well, the ups and
downs is wonderful; my old master's sons, the one
is a counter-hopper, and the other a private in the
53rd. He went to the dogs, he did, and here am
I, Edward Finch, Esquire, J.P., and owner of
Withefell Hall. Life's strange, ain't it, Miss
Beryl ?"

"I wish you would not, Beryl," said Miss Molozane; and then Mr. Geith knew in a minute that
Mr. Finch was the individual who had aspired to
Miss Molozane's hand, and whom Beryl had said she
should prefer to Dick Elsenham.

"And would Beryl have done so?" George asked
himself. Would not the polish, slight though it
might be, have been better to the girl than the
frightful vulgarity of the other's address? With
Mr. Finch he felt inclined to shout out, " Life's
strange, ain't it ?" and to wonder what there was
in it real and true.

"Do you remember, Beryl, the Sunday you and I were turned out of Withefell Church?" asked Dick, with a malicious twinkle in his black eyes.

"Yes; and I remember with satisfaction the handful of hair I pulled out of your head before we were turned out," retorted Beryl, viciously.

"What had you been doing?" asked Mr. Geith.

"It was one Sunday, when we were little children," answered Beryl; "and as we were both horribly tired of being at the Park doing nothing, we stole out, and trotted off to Withefell Church, across the fields. Nobody there knew who we were, and when Dick and I got fighting over which should have the hymn-book, we were taken out; but not before we had made a frightful noise with rolling off the seat. I was carried out, I believe, and carried home. One thing I do recollect, that I scratched Dick's face; and I sometimes wish I was young enough to scratch it again." And Beryl pulled a grimace at her cousin.

"You may make the most of your time," he said, "for you won't dare do that when Granny comes."

"I wish both you and your Granny were in the

bottom of the sea," remarked Beryl; "why don't you keep her in London? we don't want her here."

"I am sure I don't," he answered. "Tell me some way of preventing her coming, and I will."

"Tell her we have small-pox—fever—cholera— what you choose. Like all good people, she is afraid of death. You will be so pleased with Granny, Mr. Geith; she is such a nice old lady, so much like her grandson."

"I declare she is not in the least like me," interrupted Mr. Elsenham.

"That is a pity, is it not, Mr. Geith? I have not one of her letters at hand, but I think I can repeat one of her epistles."

"Do you wish me to leave the room?" asked Miss Molozane.

"I am quite indifferent," answered Beryl, as she took up a piece of paper lying on the table, and began, after clearing her throat:

"MY DEAR NIECE,—It seems to me a long time since I heard from you, but I trust your silence does not proceed from any other cause than that of having been more agreeably occupied than in writing to an old woman. I shall trust to hear you, your dear papa, Beryl, and Louisa are well.

"I hope to see you, *if perfectly convenient* (D.V.), on Monday next. Thankful as I am and ought to be to the Lord for his unspeakable mercies, I still feel I am getting old, and that an occasional change, and intercourse with young people is desirable. Will you therefore write, *by return*, saying whether you can receive me, Mr. Elsenham, Gibbs and Walton. The remainder of the servants can remain *as usual* at the 'Stag.'

"With kind remembrances to your father, Beryl, and Louisa, and much love for yourself,

"Your affectionate grandmother,

"M. L. ELSENHAM."

"L stands for Lucretia," explained Beryl, as she paused; "and I ought, perhaps, further to state that——"

"Cannot you let her alone while she is in London?" interrupted Mr. Elsenham; "and go and put on your bonnet, and let us get off to church."

"You are so fond of church, Dick."

"I'd like it better if there were any pretty girls in the parish," retorted her cousin. Whereupon

Miss Molozane rebuked them both; Mr. Elsenham for making the remark, and Beryl for provoking it. "The house is really like a bear-garden, with the two of you in it," observed the beauty.

"What is a bear-garden, Tilly?" asked Louisa gravely; but Miss Molozane declined giving any explanation; rather preferring to follow her cousin's advice. and prepare for their walk.

It was pleasant going to church across the fields in the evening, but George did not much care for the path as they came back. For one thing, the days were beginning to draw in, and, for another, the sky was cloudy and dull, seeming to threaten rain.

Altogether there was a gloom over the landscape which depressed him, and the company of Messrs. Finch and Werne, who were so good as to walk back most of the way with the Dower House party, did not tend to raise his spirits. At every step he seemed to hear the chink of gold; every sentence reminded him that these men had made their money whilst he was still struggling. Houses, lands, wealth, position, he reflected, lay waiting for the acceptance of Mr. Molozane's daughters.

Bitterly he remembered that these people would

be walking across the green Hertfordshire fields, and talking to the girls who had taught him what a happy home was like, in the (to him) dreary days to come, when he had done his work, and spoken his farewells, and returned to the old drudgery again.

He had no right to repine, certainly: he had been happy, he had enjoyed himself, his health was re-established, he had gained strength and fresh vigour through breathing the pure country air. Why, then, should he grieve? and George caught at the leaves of the trees, and plucked them off ruthlessly as he asked himself this question.

Why should he grieve? Ah, friends and fellow-travellers! how often are we asked this question? how often do we put it ourselves, and how seldom can we return any satisfactory answer to it? We have had our cake, we have eaten it. There has been no bitter in it; to the last crumb we have found it sweet. Why grieve, then? for we cannot eat and have.

But who does not grieve, who does not sorrow, for that passing away which is, after all, the real misery of life? Friends, youth, beauty, fame,

happiness, hours, where the sun is streaming on us,
moments when in the moonlight we look at faces
which we love, days which are full of such happiness that they seem scarcely to have been spent
on earth; all these we touch, to feel they are but
part of a procession which is ever moving from us,
ever passing away. Why should we grieve? Good
heavens! how could we do otherwise, when we
know so well that after the sunshine comes gloom
—after the day, night? Is it marvellous that,
feeling the darkness creeping on, we should linger
to the last in the light? that, feeling the waves of
the cruel ocean we have breasted licking our feet,
we should stretch out our hands after the groups
that are walking away over the pleasant sands we
shall never tread more?

Life's days are so gloomy when the summer is
gone, its streets are so deserted when the gallant
cavalcade is past, its ways are so stony when we
have to tread them alone, that it is no wonder we
grieve when the hour comes for parting, and the
sad good-byes are spoken; no wonder, even though
we have had all our right, our holiday, our cake,
our milk.

George Geith had had his holiday, his happy

sunshiny days of leisure ; but behold! the holidays
were well-nigh spent, and he was going back to
resume his old low place in the school of life.

He was in bad spirits; he was dull; he was
cross, if you will; and Beryl's cheerfulness vexed
him, even though that cheerfulness was evinced in
disagreeing with Mr. Werne, and laughing at his
opinions.

For once before the Withefell saint Beryl was
not demure; and when she was running most
counter to all his ideas, she would look over to
Mr. Geith for approval, which, as she was annoying
Mr. Werne for the sake of pleasing Mr. Geith, I
think she deserved.

But George would not be appeased—not even
when they got upon the question of the millennium,
concerning the time of which Beryl expressed her
belief that the Withefell vicar must have recently
had some secret information from above.

" Because, how otherwise," said the young lady,
"could he know for certain that it would be three
years hence exactly ?"

" I must say his arguments was very convinc-
ing," here put in Mr. Finch.

" You don't mean though, I suppose, that you

believe there will be an end of all things at the end of three years ?" said Beryl.

"I believe we are living in remarkable times," answered Mr. Finch, who pronounced the word as if it were "remarkyble ;" "and that we cannot tell the day nor the hour, and that therefore, as Mr. Wilton says, we ought to put our houses in order."

"But Mr. Wilton says we do know the day and hour," interposed Louisa, "for he declared that, reading the signs of the times, the end of the world would come at the expiration of three years exactly."

"For which reason," added Beryl, a little flippantly, "if it were not for death, which really may come at any minute, we needn't be in such a hurry about our houses till nearer the time."

"Do you know," said Mr. Werne, "it appears to me the service has not benefited us much."

"I am sure it has not benefited me," answered Miss Molozane ; "for I was bored to death, and I have got a chill from the damp of the church. Mr. Finch you really ought to build a new one; it is enough to kill any one sitting in it for a couple ot hours."

"It lies in such a hollow," explained Mr. Werne.

"There are plenty of nice sites in the neighbourhood," observed Beryl.

"How does it happen you don't express no opinions about the sermon, sir?" asked Mr. Finch, turning benignly towards George.

"I am one of those happy individuals who have no opinions," replied the accountant.

"Oh! Mr. Geith, when you know you are a long way towards Rome," said Miss Molozane; while Louisa followed with—

"Yes, indeed, Mr. Werne; he goes far beyond the Wattisbridge people. He does not think the service there is performed properly at all."

"He wants a procession of priests, crosses, and candles; and he would feel happier if he could go to confession," added Beryl.

"Miss Beryl, as usual, is sacrificing her acquaintances to her love of amusement," answered Mr. Geith; whilst Mr. Werne turned towards him with a curious expression in his face—an expression, the meaning of which George did not understand till afterwards.

"But about the church," said Beryl, coming back to the point from which Mr. Finch had diverged. "Won't you build one? pray do. It would involve ever so much gaiety, and we want some excitement. Let me see; there would be the stone-laying, and the opening, and we might have a few bazaars; and then whoever was married in it first, ought to invite everybody in the parish to the wedding."

"I suppose you would like a dance on the green at the consecration of the graveyard?" said Dick Elsenham

"I should like a dance anywhere, under any circumstances," returned Beryl. "It is nearly as long a thing as I can remember, being at a party. Mr. Finch, I really think I should be better pleased if you were to give a ball, than if you were to build a church."

"Now it's curious, ain't it," remarked Mr. Finch to the company generally, "that I was just a-thinking of giving a hop."

"How enchanting!" exclaimed Beryl. "Do tell us all about it. Won't you have the dancing in the picture-gallery, and——"

"I believe, Miss Molozane, I must say good evening," here interposed Mr. Werne; and shaking hands with all the party, he turned off across Molozane Park to his own residence.

Heaven knows what thoughts he carried with him by the way; but, judging from the look wherewith he regarded Beryl at parting, they could not have been pleasant.

"There is a mark against your name, old fellow," said Mr. Elsenham to Mr. Geith, looking after the retreating figure. "Werne will set you down as a Jesuit, and gravely remonstrate with my uncle on the danger of having you in the house."

"He is welcome," answered George. "I shall not be long in it now, at any rate;" and the pair walked on in silence, listening to Beryl teazing Mr. Finch to death about the ball, insisting he should fix a time, and earnestly intreating him to come to the Dower House and talk over the preliminaries.

"Grandmamma will be with us to-morrow," said Beryl, demurely. "She will be so glad to see you."

"Thank you. I shall be very pleased to call on Mrs. Elsenham; very so, indeed; and if these gentlemen will come up and eat their mutton with me on Tuesday—dine in a plain way—I shall be better pleased still. I am very sorry, sir, not to have made your acquaintance earlier," he added, turning

to George : " I should like to have a chat with you
about the City. I'm from the City myself, sir, and
I'm not ashamed to say so to nobody."

To which speech what answer could Mr. Geith
make, but that he saw no occasion for anything but
pride in the recollection ?

"And you'll come too, won't you," continued
Mr. Finch, turning towards Mr. Elsenham, which
Dick assured him he would, stating for a reason
after they parted from the owner of Withefell
Hall, "that his wine was tip-top, although his
grammar was the devil."

"Shall I tell you what your mutton will be, Mr.
Geith ?" asked Beryl. "Fish and mock turtle ;
ducks and green peas ; lamb and mint sauce ; *entrées*
innumerable ; puddings by the score ; every vege-
table you can mention ; every fruit you can imagine.
And his sister—oh! I must show you Miss Finch
when we get home. And in the way of wines, he
will give you what he calls ' clarick ' and ' mussel ;'
and white and red ; and heavy and light ; and he
will tell you that he himself does not care for anything but port ; that there was a time when he
knew more about gin and 'Old Tom' than any
genteel swallow ; and that he ain't sure but a good

glass of Hollands still beats Mounseer and Cava-
lero into fits."

"I do not intend, however, Miss Beryl, to drink
Mr. Finch's wine, and make fun of him afterwards," remarked Mr. Geith, a little ill-humouredly.

"Don't, then," said Beryl; "but, as I do not care
for either hock or claret, I shall make fun of him
if I please. It's a good soul, though. I like Mr.
Finch. He is a great favourite of mine."

"Heaven preserve me, then, from that distinction," murmured George, devoutly.

"But he is not one of my friends," she said, in
a lower tone—a tone which came back to him often
when the future became the present. "You have
disapproved of my being grave, Mr. Geith; were you
graciously pleased to approve of me this evening?"

"It is not for me to express an opinion," he
replied.

"But it is, if you form one," she answered. "I
am vexed now that I annoyed Mr. Werne. He
is better than anybody else I know; but I was in
a teazing mood, and I thought you did not care for
me to be in earnest; and so I have fallen between
two stools, as most people do when they try to
please their neighbours."

"I hope you have not hurt yourself much," said her companion; and though Beryl could not help laughing, the tears came into her eyes whilst she laughed. Pity it was getting so dark that George could not see them!

But without seeing them, he began that night taking himself to task. Sitting by the open window, inhaling the perfumes that came floating to him from the garden, alone, in the stillness, he commenced that personal cross-examination in which so few have the courage to persevere.

What did all this grief mean? What was this tearing at his heart? Why was he afraid to look forward? Why had he been so unutterably happy with these girls? He had never admired Beryl; he knew he did not now care for Matilda; whilst, as for Louey! Setting Matilda and Louey out of the question, however, thinking of a woman not as of a picture, but as a friend and companion, was not it Beryl he sorrowed to leave?—Beryl, who now occupied a shrine in his heart which had never been filled before by woman? For, though he had admired many; though he had all his life been a worshipper of beauty; though he had acknowledged may queens, fluttered around many a flame, he had never before felt anything like this —this which was eating into his soul, making existence insupportable, the future intolerable without her.

Through the long hours he sat thinking of this new gospel, which he had fancied was an old one with him, pondering over the mystery of this strange sensation which had stolen upon him so gently, so tranquilly, that it had become a part of himself before he dreamed of danger.

And now, when he saw the danger, what then ? Did he resolve to win and to wear: did he ever, even in fancy, see Beryl his wife—hear her call him husband.

Never once; for there are some pains which bring with them partial numbness; and this agony of hopeless love, of love which could but love and leave, left him no strength for aught save the thought, that he must 'go away; that at all hazards he must break the spell; and depart, carrying his wound with him.

He had never been able to realize Beryl married; even in his jealousy, even when he imagined she was lending a too favourable ear to Mr. Werne, he had never pictured her mistress of the Park;

and now, when he came to understand that without her his life would be lonely for ever, he still could not fancy this girl a wife; no delusive picture of domestic happiness arose out of the darkness to mock him with false hopes.

And, supposing the choice to have been presented to him, of living on in his present paradise, or of taking his Eve out of it into the wide world beyond, I think George Geith would have chosen the former without an instant's hesitation.   Fenced round by the hedges of Dower House; wandering amongst the roses in its old-fashioned garden; standing in the twilight on the terrace; he had felt secure both from sorrow and sin.   The past lay outside, the future was forgotten.   His long servitude, his seven years of work, his nights of toil, his days of anxiety, were all left behind when once the dear old house was reached, when once kindly voices greeted him, and soft hands touched his in welcome.

There was no need to think of money, no necessity for planning about ways and means; and to many a man it takes the gloss off love to have to be thinking about pounds, shillings, and pence; about sirloins of beef and legs of mutton, and that little account of the baker's, which he foresees the blessing of a wife will entail upon him. Love-making is a pleasanter occupation than calculating "how much a year." Somehow, computing the expense of a woman's keep destroys the idea of her divinity. The business view of matrimony is not a pleasant one; but that romantic affection which in the full enjoyment of to-day, forgets that there must come a to-morrow, is a foretaste of heaven in which to-day is for ever, and to-morrow and the end never.

It is a mistake, I think, to imagine that a man's thoughts rush off straight from love to marriage, from ideality to reality. On the contrary, it appears to me natural that most men should ignore the mainland, with its labour, its care, its responsibility, so long as they can float over the ocean of love without trouble, without fear.

Moreover, if the acme of misery be the inability to hope, the acme of happiness is surely the absence of any wish to hope, of anything to wish for, save this, that the present might go on for ever without change.

And this was the state of beatitude in which George Geith had been living, and from which he

wakened with a start to tell himself he must go.
For what was he to Beryl, and what could Beryl
Molozane be to him, save a memory of happiness?
In the dull, dull days to come, when the snow was
on the ground, when the frost was lying on the
graves in Fen Court, when the black trees were
dripping with blacker rain, and the pavements
were sloppy, and the City wretched, he should
still in recollection see Beryl standing among the
roses, still hear her laugh ringing out happy and
mirthful as of yore. To him she would never grow
old; to him there would be no awful hereafter of
grey hair, of wrinkles, of old youngness, of sickness, feebleness, loss of youth. She would be his
young love to him for ever; his to the day of his
death, the laughing, singing, gleeful Beryl, of
sweet seventeen. Other men might see their
brides change to matrons, but for him there would
be no change. She would be in his memory just
the same, for ever and for ever.

Shall I go on telling how through the night he
sat hugging his misery to him; indulging in melancholy, and finding sweetness in the cup, as though
he were still a boy, and young enough to find imaginary luxury in a draught he had never tasted?

Shall I repeat the old, old story, of how first love—first, though it come as the finish to fifty fancies, hath still power to strike off the iron bands of time, and leave the soul free from the incubus of the years that have aged and worn the body. Would it not weary the reader to tell of the mist of tears through which this strong man beheld his ship going down among the breakers; to describe how, with head bent forward and arms folded on the window-sill, he made his discovery, and decided on his future course, whilst the gloom deepened and darkened, and wrapped him lovingly and gently in the clouds of night?

He was unmanned, and it was well that there were none who could see his face, for of all the troubles he had met and surmounted no trouble had ever come nigh unto him like this.

And yet, if he could have retraced his steps, would he? Ah! who that has loved would choose his ways to have been different? Who, after eating of the tree of the knowledge of good and evil, would go back into Eden and leave the fruit untasted?

' Amongst thorns and brambles his future way may lie, for his sake the ground may be cursed, and the earth yield her increase only in sorrow and with pain.

All this matters not, for his eyes have been opened, and it is something, even when wandering through all earth's darkest places, for him to remember that he has once caught a glimpse of heaven!

CHAPTER VII.

A LITTLE SURPRISE.

How many good resolutions which night hears made, does not morning see broken? what does not wear a different aspect at noontide, from that which it did at midnight? What course decided on in the darkness do we not modify in the light? Are we the same men and the same women, I marvel, as the clock chimes the early morning hours, as we were when they were striking in the starlight stillness? Or are we like the lady of the fairy tale, who was a true wife one half of her time and a wandering wolf the other?

If night's good resolves could be carried into action after sunrise on the morrow, what a perfect world we should live in. If sluggards could but rise at the first call; if the weak could be but as strong; if the strong could be but as forbearing when day breaks as they meant to be a few hours before, would not our neighbours be almost too good? would not our own virtues dazzle our eyes? If ever the time arrives when that is done in the morning which was decided on over night, there will be no more stories to write of weakness, sorrow, repentance, remorse. The world will be peopled with saints, and our bookshelves will be full of the lives thereof!

But as matters stand at present, the pie-crusts on which we expend so much labour in solitude are broken as soon as we come face to face with the world and its temptations. It was so with George Geith at any rate. The Beryl thought of in the midst of night's solemnity was a different being to the Beryl he met glancing amongst the flowers. She was something in the one case to part from, to beware of, as a snare and a sorrow; whilst in the other she was a girl to see as much of as possible; to be near, to talk to, to laugh with, as long as circumstances would permit.

The night had bid him depart; the sunshine begged him to stay. The still voice of the darkness had said, " Go; for each hour will but increase the misery of the inevitable parting;" but the summer wind murmured pleasanter words, as it fanned his cheek caressingly, and whispered, "Be happy whilst you may; your stay can do no harm to anybody but yourself."

What man would not have hearkened to the latter voice, and still basked on in the sunshine, more particularly when it seemed as if that morning, beyond all other mornings, Beryl had laid herself out to be agreeable and winning? She had her dogs with her on the lawn, where the poodle marched about gravely on his hind legs, and Royal offered first his right and then his left paw to George, with a sublime gravity which was irresistibly ludicrous.

From the lawn they walked up the elm avenue, and as they walked Beryl spoke of her father and sisters with a pretty gravity which was amazingly becoming to her.

Had not Mr. Geith noticed how ill papa was looking? Could he, would he, tell her how affairs were likely to turn out? Should they be able to keep the Park? To which latter question George made answer that he could not exactly tell her yet; but he inquired, "if it were to be sold, would Mr.

Elsenham not purchase it, and so keep the property in the family?"

"He could not," Beryl replied; "he has not sixpence in the world of his own. Granny wanted to buy it, but papa would not sell. She then wished to rent it, but he preferred letting it to Mr. Werne."

"Would Mrs. Elsenham not purchase it for her grandson?" George inquired.

"No; and if she would, I am sure papa could never bear to see Dick master of the Park."

"Does he not like him?" asked her companion.

"Have you lived all this time with us, and not found that out?" she retorted. "Papa likes Dick almost as well as I do."

"But, seriously, you appear to me excellent friends."

"Do we?" she said; "that show how much appearances may mislead."

"Do you mean then that you really are not friends? From what you said about Mr. Elsenham, I expected to find him an intolerable puppy. I confess I have been agreeaby disappointed in him, and ——"

"And you think Tilly has chosen wisely," she

added; "Well, Mr. Geith, if that be your opinion, it is not mine. You do not know Dick; you have never seen him yet in a fair light. I would not be in Dick's power, I would not be at the mercy of his generosity for any earthly consideration. I would rather be indebted to Granny, and that is saying all I can say."

"If Mr. Molozane dislikes him, why does he permit the marriage to go on?"

"Now, Mr. Geith, do you think he could stop it if Granny and Tilly have set their hearts on its taking place? Besides, if Tilly likes him—and she does, I suppose—is not that all we need care for? Sometimes I can't hold my tongue about him to her, but afterwards I could bite it out for my pains."

"I should like to know why you dislike him so much, whilst you appear to get on so well together."

"It is very likely you will have your desire gratified if you go with him to the Hall to-morrow evening," she said, significantly, colouring a little as she spoke. "You have seen Dick at his very best, I assure you; and as for our getting on well, I have never yet met with anybody I could not talk to, except Granny; and even Louey is afraid

of her. Louey will take to her writing as if she
were earning ten thousand a year when Mrs.
Elsenham comes."

" Do you think your sister would show me any
of her writing ?" he asked.

" To be sure she would, and be pleased at anybody taking an interest about the matter. I was
looking at some of her things the other day, and I
really do think they are very strange and wonderful, if I could understand them ; but then I never
was in the least clever. Now, I think Tilly, who
is, might read Louey's poems to please her."

" Does Mr. Molozane not read them ?"

" I think I told you we had lost one sister," she
said ; and the explanation was satisfactory. " I will
ask Louey for some of her poems." And straight
away darted Beryl, followed at full flight by the
dogs, who went growling and rolling over each
other as they sped after her.

I am afraid George anathematized the manuscripts. It is very nice to be literary, and to talk
on intellectual subjects may be very interesting
and improving to those who care about intellect ;
but a walk, for all that, in the clear bright air of a
summer morning, with a pretty, lively girl for a

companion—a girl, moreover, with whom one is secretly in love—is nicer and more interesting still.

" Hang the poems !" thought the accountant, as he retraced his steps towards the house ; and who may blame him ?

" She is busy now," said Beryl, when she returned ; "but she will look you some out after breakfast. She was so pleased about your wanting to see them, Mr. Geith ! Somehow, I do not think we are right about Louey. It cannot be good for anybody to live a life apart, as she does ; can it ?"

" I think, if she were my sister, I should try to understand her a little," answered George.

" I wish I could ; I wish I was clever !" sighed Beryl. " Now, if she would write prose, I should be able to read her things ; but poetry—oh, if you could but imagine how it wearies me ! If you do think her rhymes foolish, Mr. Geith, I am sure I need not ask you not to tell her so. She is hardly more than a child yet, though she does scribble on constantly."

And the tears sprang into Beryl's eyes as she spoke, though from what secret well they gushed George could not imagine. He only knew that

K 2

this quick sensitiveness, this April nature, which was for ever changing, where there was sunshine one moment and shade the next, was one of Beryl's greatest charms.

He was beginning to understand how slight a line divides mirth from melancholy; how quickly tears may dim eyes that have been a moment before dancing with merriment. He was commencing to learn wherein this girl's power of attraction lay, viz., in a mental constitution which combined the keenest sense of the ridiculous, with the deepest sympathy for suffering; which, while it could see something ludicrous in the most ordinary—ay, and it might be, in the saddest circumstances of every-day life—had yet every chord attuned to echo the slightest breath of trouble, the faintest sigh of woe. If the finest wit be near akin to the deepest wisdom; so, the extremest gaiety is next-door neighbour to the truest sorrow; and those people who in themselves combine the two opposites of light-heartedness and sadness, charm us as the Irish melodies charm us, we scarcely know why, till we learn the secret of their peculiarity, which is, that plaintive minors are ever mingling with joyous majors; and that wherever a ringing octave comes, we may be sure a melancholy seventh will succeed thereto.

Thinking of this, thinking of what strange creatures women are, and of how much stranger some women are than others, George got fairly addled after breakfast among his accounts, and for once he was not sorry to see Louisa entering the library, and Louisa, moreover, without her cap.

He was so astonished at the change in her appearance, that for a minute he could not take his eyes off her.

" Do you not think it an improvement?" said the young lady, who, like Beryl, was not very easily disconcerted; though, like Beryl, she blushed a little as she spoke.

" I should think I do," he answered. " What can have induced you to disfigure yourself for so long a time?"

" My hair is only just growing again," she laughed, touching her short silky locks; " but I thought I should like to put on my best looks for Granny. Here are my manuscripts, Mr. Geith. Beryl said you would take the trouble of reading them;" and she straightway laid down the papers, and walking across the room, took up her old position on the library steps.

"Are you going to read them?" she asked, surveying him calmly from her vantage-ground.

"What! now?" he said.

"Certainly, now, this minute. I want to see what you think of them. I shall know better from your face than from any words you may speak."

It was a pleasant announcement certainly; but still George did not shrink from the task. He had voluntarily undertaken it; and if the manuscripts had to be read, and read moreover in the presence of the author, why, they should be read, that was all!

Besides, he really was curious to see what Louisa could find to say about things in general, and men and women in particular; and, accordingly, he opened the first folio which came to his hand, and which proved to be a tragedy in five acts, written out—as the productions of young authors always are written out—so legibly, with such loving neatness, that a printer might weep regretful tears over them.

For a while George read on steadily, then he began to lift his eyes from the page and look towards the author doubtfully. Meantime she sat

perfectly still on the top of the steps, with her
elbows resting on her knees, and her chin supported with both hands, staring at him with the
most absorbed air of contemplation imaginable.

She would have been a proud girl at that
minute, could she have known exactly what was
passing through his mind. For it had suddenly
dawned upon him, what some creatures in their
teens can write before they die!

There was not much in the story, perhaps, and
certainly nothing original in its treatment.

A father wrongfully executed; a son vowing
himself to revenge; a woman faithful in love, yet
strong in duty; the scene laid in the remotest
Saxon ages; there was little in all this to interest
a man like George Geith, and yet he was interested in the authoress and astonished at her
talent.

He was sufficient of a critic to be able to sift out
the corn from the chaff; and as he came upon such
a passage as this:

"Revenge!
It is the fire which passion strikes from vice,"

he could not help marvelling where, in the name of
wonder, the girl had gathered her ideas from.

On and still on he read :

"Go to; I feel not love : 'twas made for fools,
   And is a worthless boon."
      "It was *my* all; I gave it *thee*."

I am copying from the original manuscript, an
I pause here to ask, what George Geith asked himself; where do these thoughts come from ? How can
people whom the breath of passion has never touched,
whom the flames of love have never scorched, imagine these things? how, when they have imagined
them, can they put them into words ?   The genius
of youth must, I think, be inspiration.   It is easy
to conceive how those who have passed through
the furnace can tell of its heat ; but it is as impossible to imagine how those who have never been
tried in the fires of love, hate, or revenge, can write
of their intensity, as to think how men who have
never trodden the shores of a foreign land can describe its scenery.

Still George read on, read conscientiously, till
he came to the last page ; then he turned over the
cover, and looked at Louisa.

"Well, Mr. Geith——?"   He could see that
the face of the Molozane Solomon was very pale as
she said this interrogatively.

"I am astonished, Miss Louisa. I did not think you could have done it. I do not know where you can have got it."

And opening the manuscript again, he looked once more over this :

> "Thou knowest not my nature :
> The babbling brook, that ever pines and frets,
> A breeze will stir; but the wide boundless ocean
> Smiles at the feeble breeze, and can be tost
> By Heaven's whirlwinds only: so my soul
> Looked on life's troubles with a placid eye,
> And bore them meekly, as what all endured,
> And the gods ordered; but the loftier storm
> Hath roused its slow-awakened energies,
> And stern and steady are they."

"You think I can write, then?" She was by this time standing beside him.

"I am certain you can."

"And shall I make money ?"

"That is a different matter; you may perhaps hereafter."

"Hereafter! when ?"

"Fifteen, twenty years, perhaps," he said.

"When papa is dead; when the Park is gone; when I shall care for nothing; when it will not signify what comes or what goes ;" and she fell on her knees beside the table, and rained such tears

over her papers as George had never previously
seen fall from a woman's eyes. Did he need to ask
then whence she got part of her inspiration? Was
he coming to understand at last that the life's
book of the youngest may hold within its pages
something of which the philosophy of the oldest
dreams not?

Had this been the vision of the child beside
him? Had she been thinking to redeem the past,
to gild the future? Had she fallen into the usual
error of imagining an ink-bottle would prove a gold
mine, and quires of foolscap an El Dorado? Had
she too built costly castles reaching to the skies?
Had she talked to her own heart of the certainty
of possibilities? In the solitude of soul into which
she seemed to have retired, had she sketched the
outline of a landscape which was never to be filled
in?

And was reality horrible after the dream?
Were those tears the sobs wherewith youth ever
mourns the first touch of the cold water of experience?

Life is so icy, its practical lessons are so stern,
that it is no marvel the young weep shudderingly
at the plunge, and look back through blinding

tears regretfully towards the bank which they can never regain.

If George had spoken at random he had spoken truly, and truth always travels straight home, for which reason Louisa fell on her knees and wept, crying over her manuscripts such tears as unhappy mothers have sometimes cause to shed over their firstborn.

If there had been joy in these things there was trouble likewise; if, after her travail, she had rejoiced, so now, because of creations which she had brought into the world, she mourned; and George was vainly essaying some word of comfort, hopelessly racking his brain for sentences of consolation, when Beryl came in, and took the office of soother upon herself.

If George Geith had wanted anything more to make him in love with the girl, her conquest would have at that moment been complete. Had the fire needed fuel there would have been sufficient heaped on it at that moment to make its flames inextinguishable.

There was a something so indescribably tender about the way she took her sister to her; it was so pitiful to see the two clinging to one another;

Beryl's sympathy was so true, her self-forgetfulness
so real; the look in her brown eyes, as she lifted
them to George's face, so vexed and troubled, that
the accountant thought he had never seen so exquisite a home picture as that pair of young
creatures seated together on the ground, with arms
twining round waist and neck, with heads touching,
with flowing dresses intermingling, and lying in
masses of light drapery over the dark-green
carpet.

"Don't cry, dear; don't cry," was all the eldest
could find to say at first; but as by degrees she
gathered from George the cause of the outburst,
she murmured better words of comfort, and
drawing, by some feminine chemistry, every dark
tint out of the future, presented it in such bright
hues for Louisa's inspection, that, as the clouds
will clear off a child's face at sight of a pleasant
picture, her tears began to cease, and her sobs to
grow less frequent.

But she never raised her head from Beryl's
shoulder; she never took her arms away from
clasping Beryl's neck; all the time she listened to
the hopeful story her sister whispered, she nestled
close to a heart which seemed strong enough and

brave enough to bear its own sorrows and another's too.

"Now, I wonder," thought George, "what Miss Molozane would have done had she been here;" and he was just considering that the beauty might not have shown herself in such an amiable light, when the door opened, and a voice which he instantly recognised from Beryl's mimicry of it, exclaimed, in tones of the most unequivocal surprise and indignation:

"Well! I'm sure."

CHAPTER VIII.

MR. RICHARD ELSENHAM.

AT sound of the well-known voice, Beryl started to her feet with a suddenness which almost threw Louisa on her face.

"Good gracious! grandmamma, how you did startle me," she cried, her cheeks all aglow.

"How you have shocked me," retorted her virtuous relative. "Beryl, when will you learn to conduct yourself like a young lady? Rise up, Louisa, and sit properly upon a chair. What are you crying about? Dry your eyes this moment, and——" with that stiffening of the back of which Beryl made such a point, "Who is this gentleman, if I may inquire?"

"That gentleman is Mr. Geith, Mrs. Elsenham,"

said Beryl, who had by this time recovered from her fright; "and—how did you come, grandmamma? how did you get in? I never heard you. Have you seen Matilda?"

" I have seen no one but yourself," answered Mrs. Elsenham. " The hall-door was open; I knocked, I rang; but, as usual, no one attended to the summons. I went into the drawing-room: it was empty. Then, hearing voices, I tried the library."

" I am very sorry," said Beryl, apologetically; " won't you come up-stairs now, and take off your bonnet? I suppose Gibbs is with you?" And Beryl manœuvred her grandmother to the door, from which point she shot back a comical glance towards George, who had remained standing from the time of Mrs. Elsenham's appearance. As for Louisa, at an early period she had effected her escape from the room; and Beryl was left to meet the storm which she knew would be sure to burst when once the door closed behind them.

" Shan't I catch it?" said the look she cast towards George, as plainly as a look could speak; and it would not be affirming too much to say that Beryl rather enjoyed the idea of the scolding, which she intended to reproduce for her friend's benefit at the earliest opportunity.

For the young lady was perfectly indifferent to anything her grandmother chose to say to her.

" Hard words break no bones," she remarked to George afterwards; " and I am, thank goodness, too old now to have my ears boxed. How that respectable relative of mine used to make them tingle !"

If scolding could have made them do so, Beryl's feelings need not have been envied; but, as she remarked, "Such a trifling thing as her grand-mother's opinion produced no effect upon her."

On George, however, Mrs. Elsenham's words of wisdom fell with the sharpness of hail. Her worldly ideas came upon him like frost in summer; and when, into his Eden this ancient serpent entered, he felt that the sooner he got out of Paradise the better it might be for him and every other person concerned.

Not all Beryl's powers of mimicry could recon-cile him to Mrs. Elsenham's peculiarities. The minutes which the young lady stole in order to tell him Granny's " latest" could not make him feel other than perfect detestation for the manner in which said Granny tracked Beryl's footsteps, and compelled her to make ignominious and hurried retreats from the library on to the terrace.

True, the minute Mrs. Elsenham re-closed the door, Beryl's face reappeared at the window; and the hiding and seeking at which the pair played, the lurking behind ivy and honeysuckles, and the triumphant flights which Beryl effected, were amazingly amusing and exciting. During the whole of his life at the Dower House, George Geith had never laughed so much as he did now at granddaughter and grandmother; but it was intolerable to have to laugh silently; and at times when Beryl was within earshot, when her last sentence was scarcely spoken, he found it almost impossible to reply to Mrs. Elsenham's inquiries with necessary gravity. What the lady suspected—whether she thought Beryl was making love to him or he to Beryl; whether she guessed Beryl was ridiculing her, or imagined she was making the accountant's stay too agreeable, George could not decide; he only knew that Mrs. Elsenham laid herself out to be unpleasant, and that in this laudable design she succeeded to perfection.

For to him her manner was insufferable. If he

had been a servant, and necessary to her comfort. or conducive to her convenience, she might have treated him with some consideration and courtesy; but, as he happened only to be a man in business, she missed no opportunity of letting him know his rung of the social ladder was very near the ground.

To George she was like a perpetual blister. It seemed as though she were trying to enter a continual protest against his presence in the house, and the feeling wherewith it pleased the owner thereof to regard him. Cordially he hated her, her maid, and her dog, a nasty, snarling, cross-grained King Charles, that always had something the matter with its throat, which rendered necessary external applications of oil, and the internal administration of cream.

"I should like to put a stone round its neck," observed George to Beryl.

"I shall kill it some day, I know," she replied; "and then if Granny can hang me for wilful murder I shall die the death."

As for Mr. Elsenham, senior, the gentleman who always travelled in his sister-in-law's company, he was a perfectly unoffending personage, who took to George amazingly, assured him he would get on, told him he had once been a City man himself, and that he had made a deal of money. " A very great deal," he added, champing his toothless jaws the while. " Ah! the City's the place, when all's said and done—and the west is very nice, and the country is very pleasant—give me the City."

And then the accountant wondered if this old man, who had money and leisure, really would like to return to a dull City office, and pore over musty books.

With the sunlight streaming over him, he forgot that the sun had almost done shining anywhere for Mr. Elsenham, and that he was looking back as he spoke to days when even a City office seemed gay and cheerful; to days when he was young, and life lay all before him.

It was funny to notice how jealous Mrs. Elsenham became of her kinsman's liking for the accountant; how constantly she interposed her portly figure between them; how frequently she bore Dives off in triumph to read good books to him, over which he fell asleep.

Beryl's description of these readings, and of the way in which Mr. Elsenham seized on any chance of escape from them, was irresistibly comic. In-

deed, what was there in those days that was not
comic, save the state of Mr. Molozane's affairs, and
the certainty that the accounts were nearly finished,
and that George's holiday was consequently almost
ended ?

One other thing also, perhaps, was not ludicrous
—a new phase of Mr. Richard Elsenham's character ;
one for which George Geith could have kicked
him from Withefell to London without wearying
of the exercise, viz., getting dead drunk when a
suitable opportunity offered, and boasting in his
cups that Beryl liked him better than she liked
anybody else on earth.

" I'd have but to hold up my finger," he hic-
cupped, as he and George walked home from
Withefell, " and—she'd—come. Matilda's not my
choice—d—— her—she's the devil's ; and if the
devil was dead, and I had her money, I'd have
Beryl ; and—" with an awful lurch, which
nearly capsized his companion—" Beryl would have
me."

" She would not," said George, provoked out of
his silence.

" She—would," affirmed her admirer ; " she likes
me better—than she does—Werne ;" and Mr.

Elsenham plumped down on the side-path, and commenced invoking blessings on his Beryl.

"Get up, you brute !" exclaimed George, and he shook his companion, who, catching his hand began maundering—

"I'm sorry for you, old fellow; I like you; you're a trump. But you mistake; you think Beryl likes you? she don't. I know Beryl, and I know—she's—a humbug."

Having vouchsafed which piece of information, Mr. Elsenham fell back into the accountant's arms.

"It would serve you right to leave you to sleep in the road," remarked Mr. Geith, while he endeavoured to steady his companion's steps.

"Beryl will—marry—Werne," proceeded Miss Molozane's *fiancé;* "when she can't have me she'll take the highest bidder. If I'd the spirit of a mouse, I'd send Matilda to the right-about, hang her, and take Beryl."

And after this statement, Mr. Elsenham began to sing "Lizzie Lindsay" at the highest pitch of his voice.

Whether it was that the thought of Lord Ronald Clanronald's happiness proved too much for him, or that the idea of George Geith's misery

touched his heart, I do not know, but when he
came to the last line of the song, which states that
the energetic young person whose adventures it re-
cords had gone off—

> "His pride and his darling to be."

Mr. Richard Elsenham commenced whimpering, and
took George entirely into his confidence.

"I'd rather see her your wife than Werne's," he
said; "Werne would not come home with me as
you are doing; Werne would send his footman with
a pair of cursed calves; Werne's a milksop; Werne's
a saint; he does not smoke, and if Beryl marries
him I'll never go and see her, I'll cut her, I'll dis-
own her, I'll be —— if I don't."

The foregoing sentence in which, as Dick Elsenham spoke it, every second word was an oath, was
jerked out by the drunken idiot as he staggered
along the path leaning on the accountant's arm.

With what feelings George Geith listened to it I
think I need not record; but as Dick proceeded to
say that Beryl was only going to marry the saint
for an establishment, and that her father had put
her up to it, and that when she was mistress of the
Park, Mr. Werne would be nowhere, his companion
grew so furious that he could not help stopping

short and shaking Mr. Elsenham till the young man had scarcely a breath left to draw.

"If you can think of nothing good to say about your relations, for God's sake hold your tongue," he exclaimed; "don't soil your cousin's name by draging it through the mire and dirt of your own nature; for if you do, I'll leave you to find your way back to the Dower House as best you can."

Whereupon Mr. Elsenham became pathetic, and entreated George not to desert him.

"I have nobody in the world," he wept, "and I'm fond of you; I love you like a brother."

"If you were my brother I'd thrash you till I was tired; I would certainly cure you of making a beast of yourself."

"It—was—all—that—claret," explained Mr. Elsenham; and he rambled on for some time about the devilish good wine that snob had in his cellar, and about what a grand thing it was for swells, that there were snobs who were glad to entertain them.

All the meanness and vulgarity of the man's nature revealed itself to George's gaze during the course of that interminable walk; all his arrogance, self-conceit, want of truth, and want of principle, were exhibited by Miss Molozane's suitor for the accountant's benefit, and he was at last provoked to say :

"If your cousin has ever seen you like this, I don't wonder at her hating you."

"Hate me! she loves me; she sits up for me; Beryl likes the ground I walk on; and I love Beryl; and she loves me. You thought, perhaps, she liked you, old fellow, but that was only because we kept it—so close—so—dark."

After that George Geith held his peace. Out of the past there came to him the proverbs once so familiar, "Answer not a fool according to his folly, lest he be wise in his own conceit." "Speak not in the ears of a fool, for he will despise the wisdom of thy words." "Though thou shouldest bray a fool in a mortar among wheat with a pestle, yet will not his foolishness depart from him."

At the moment, I am afraid the accountant wished he had the braying of that lump of folly, laziness, conceit, and arrogance, which he had the felicity of escorting back to the Dower House, where, exactly as Mr. Elsenham had said, Beryl was sitting up for them.

"I—told—you so," said her cousin, with drunken

gravity, propping himself up against one corner of the hall, and shaking his head solemnly at George, who could scarcely resist laughing at the figure the man presented. "Beryl—ain't you—fond of me?"

"No, I am not," answered Beryl; "and if you do not go to bed at once I shall tell Granny about you to-morrow."

"You may tell the—devil," retorted Mr. Elsenham, and he thrust his hands into his pockets; and surveyed his cousin with an idiotic smile.

"Wait—till—tell—you Beryl; we had sthunning —dinner—and I made—myself—pleasant—to Miss Finch."

"I wish you were married to her," said Beryl, in an audible aside.

"And Werne was there—and—con—dicted me —and if—you take him Beryl, I'll—never be friends with you—never."

At which stage, Mr. Elsenham's hat, that had previously been very much on one side, fell off; and whilst he was vainly attempting to pick it up, Beryl took the opportunity of asking Mr. Geith to get him to go to bed.

It was by no means a difficult task, for being almost too tipsy to be troublesome, he suffered

George to help him up-stairs, where, after a vain attempt to pull off a very tight pair of boots, George left him to his fate.

"Does Miss Molozane know?" the accountant could not help asking Beryl next morning.

"Of course she does; she has seen him what he calls 'happy' often enough. Oh! indeed Dick is a very nice young man, and will make an admirable husband."

Which answer, and the indignant sarcasm of Beryl's manner as she spoke it, caused Mr. Geith to reflect, as he travelled from St. Margaret's to London, that it was a more difficult thing for girls to get married to their minds than he had once supposed.

Given, for instance, the Molozanes. The two eldest could certainly settle well if they chose, but then, would that settling be at all to their satisfaction? He saw how hard it would be for them to meet with exactly the suitable person. Situated as they were, they could scarcely hope to unite love and competence, or competence and love. They might in one sense make great matches, secure husbands who could at once raise them to affluence, and give them every advantage to which their birth entitled them. The sets-off against those matches were the impossibility of such girls really and truly loving the husbands who thus endowed them with all manner of worldly possessions; the differences of opinion, and taste, that would be certain to arise; and in Matilda's case the tortures, consequent on his vulgarity, to which she would be subjected if she were to discard her cousin, and marry Mr. Finch.

That she had chosen that which she believed the lesser evil, George could well understand; and although he now cordially detested Mr. Richard Elsenham, he could not but admit that perhaps, considering her nature, she had chosen wisely.

But how would it be with Beryl? In all honesty, putting himself and his own personal feelings out of the question, how would it fare with her if she married Mr. Werne?

Would she—could she—ever settle down into a suitable wife for a grave, good, sensible man, for whom she did not feel one atom of affection? Would not the dull, decorous life kill her? Would she not sicken of the poor, weary of her wealth, die of the Sundays, despair through the week? Could she ever get fond—really fond—of one so utterly her opposite.   As she matured, if she ever did mature, would not the gap widen?   Would not he get more solemn—she more eager for gaiety, more impatient of control?

Would not that love which George felt satisfied she had to give to some one, prove her curse sooner or later?

But there George stopped.   Beyond her marriage, if she did marry, there lay a desert of years over which he never could fancy her light feet journeying.

Just the same then, as previously, he found he could not imagine Beryl married—Beryl staid.

For a moment he let himself try to picture his circumstances altered, and her his wife; but he found he could not realize that.

The only dream he was able to conceive true, was this: that for some reason or other he might have always to be coming and going to and from the Dower House; and that as he went and came he should always find Beryl there, and Beryl still the same.

In that waking dream the summer was perpetual; he saw no dark wintry days, he beheld no snow on the ground, no leafless trees tossing their branches to the stormy sky. The fields were ever green, the waters were ever clear; the flowers never faded; men and women never grew old. No sorrow entered into that vision; no tears dimmed bright eyes; no warm hearts changed and grew cold; no tones wearied; no harsh words were uttered; all faces wore perpetual smiles.

There was no thought of parting, no mention of farewell; and the man, best portion of whose life had been spent in facing all manner of stern realities, gave himself up to the fascination of his dreams, and letting his sense sleep whilst he perfected it, went wandering on through Elysian fields, till the engine, rushing with a snort, and a shriek, and a whistle, into the Shoreditch station, brought him back to the life which it was his duty and his interest to live with all his energies awake.

"Was I dreaming of heaven?" he thought, as he passed out with the crowd, and walked down Bishopsgate Street, and thence across St. Mary Axe, bearing steadily towards Fen Court.

CHAPTER IX.

BACK TO TOWN.

IT is curious that there should always be such a grievous *quid* placed against the *quo* of even our most innocent pleasures; that so surely as a man leaves his business and enjoys the shortest possible period of recreation, he should find on his return things going wrong; disagreeable letters piled on his desk, containing imperative demands from duns, announcements of suspensions, or perhaps intelligence that some friendly neighbour has been doing his best to damage his connection by going round to his customers, or tampering with his clients.

Whether it is that the change from freedom to anxiety makes a man less fitted to bear these annoyances patiently, or that the troubles of every day, instead of being met and cleared away before closing time each evening, are thus accumulated in one formidable heap, I can scarcely tell; all I know is, that the first day at home, or at office, after a long absence, is detestable; it is a man's sorrowful return to school after the holidays; it is extra lessons and additional punishments, from sunrise to sunset.

George Geith found it disagreeable, at any rate, for he had been in town for a few hours on the previous Friday, and now it was only Wednesday in the following week; but still, in that short time, he discovered that business had not been going well, and that he must never take so long a holiday for the future.

Mr. Foss was ill, to commence with; he had known that, but he had depended on his other clerk keeping close to the office, and attending to customers, instead of which it appeared that his other clerk had taken holiday too, and that all persons who climbed up to his door had been solaced with the very definite information that he would "Return in an hour," which they derived from a small card hung on the panel. How many customers had been offended during his few days of absence? How many had come back at the expiration of an hour, half-a-dozen times, and then

departed, never to return, it would be useless to
tell. Everything was wrong, everything in confusion. Letters that ought to have been attended to
were lying unopened; notices that should have
been seen to, were resting peacefully on his desk.

Had he been at Fen Court during the whole of
the previous week, it is more than probable he
would not have done a stroke of fresh business,
but as he chanced to be away, fresh business had
poured in to be neglected.

Hanging up his hat, and putting on his office
coat, the accountant, without wasting an unnecessary second in vain regrets, got to work. He was
clear of the Dower House now, and could work;
and the amount of business he managed to get
through that morning proved a surprise even to
himself.

"So you're back at last," said Mr. Bemmidge,
opening the door of the inner office, and greeting
George with a grasp which made the accountant's
fingers tingle. "I was thinking of going down to
see whether you were living or dead, or if you
were going to set up in business at that outlandish
place where you've been staying."

"I have often been here, though you have not

seen me," answered his friend; "and I called at your office not ten days since; but your clerk said you had gone to Brighton."

"So I had; Mrs. B. and the children are all down there. I ran down from Saturday till Monday. "Lor' bless you, I can't take such holidays as you do. I can't stay away for a month at a time, and only pay angels' visits to my office. I was saying to my wife, Hertfordshire must surely hold some great attraction for you. Eh! is that it?"

"The attraction of hard work," answered the hypocrite, "which is enough to take me anywhere. And the worst of it is, the work is not finished yet; and how I am ever to get it finished I do not know."

"Well, I must say you look as if the work had agreed with you," observed Mr. Bemmidge, stepping back in order to obtain a better view. "You are worth twenty of the man you were in the early part of the summer. If you want to insure your life, now's the time."

"What should I want to insure my life for? I have neither kith nor kin."

"But it is never too late to repair that. We

have all been expecting to hear of your marriage this fortnight past. Mrs. B. said she was certain— nothing but a lady could be keeping you so long out of town."

"Which shows how little Mrs. Bemmidge knows of me," replied George. "Years and years ago I married business, and I have seen nothing, so far, that could make me unfaithful to my choice—nothing certainly in Hertfordshire;" and George uttered this untruth with an appearance of the frankest sincerity.

"Well, I am glad you have had the change, at any rate; you look a hundred per cent. the better for it; and I dare say you feel a new creature."

"It has certainly done me a great deal of good," George replied; "but health has been purchased too dearly in this instance, I am afraid. Being out of town has done my business harm."

"But you were at work in the country, you say?"

"Yes; but work in the country never pays like work in town. To be sure," added George, carelessly, "it may bring new town work, for Mr. Finch—Finch & Cross, you know, of Fore-street —has promised to send me what business he can."

"Edward Finch!" exclaimed Mr. Bemmidge.

"If you can get into his good books your fortune's made."

"And I have also met Mr. Werne, head partner in that great druggist's house in Little Britain; you know the firm I mean; and he says he can put a good deal in my way, so that, altogether, perhaps my visit to Hertfordshire may not prove quite unproductive."

And George uttered this sentence, looking straight into Mr. Bemmidge's face, and speaking as if during the entire time of his absence he had never spared a thought for anything but business.

Heavens! what deceivers we are! How calmly we go on cheating ourselves and our neighbours, till even those who know us best can hardly tell which part of our lives is true, and which false. Had Beryl Molozane heard George Geith talking to his friend, she would really have fancied all he had thought of at the Dower House was his fee, and extending his connection; and she would have turned away heartsick at the idea, that all their pleasant hours he had deemed wasted; that all their happy holiday was considered unproductive, save in so far as it brought him into contact with two good City men.

M 2

As for Mr. Bemmidge, he was enchanted to hear of the good company in which his friend had found himself, and he had no hesitation in expressing his surprise at how George had "got at them."

"There is no mystery in the matter," said the accountant; "Mr. Werne is a tenant, and Mr. Finch a neighbour, of the gentleman for whom I have been doing business. In the country, you know, great people are not so inaccessible as they seem to be in the City."

"I wish I could meet with some of these nobs, and get a good order for wine out of them," said Mr. Bemmidge, perfectly unconscious that a sneer had lain hidden in the last part of the accountant's sentence.

"I wish you could, if it would help your balance at the end of the year," said George; but he thought, as he spoke of Mr. Finch's wines, and felt assured Mr. Bemmidge's primest seals would not be given house-room.

It had long been the accountant's opinion, that his friend did not know good wine from bad, and he could not help smiling as he contrasted the fearful decoctions which Mr. Bemmidge had pronounced first-rate, with the pure products of choice vintages wherewith Mr. Finch made expiation for his sins of grammar.

"Something seems to be amusing you," said Mr. Bemmidge, with the air of a man ready to take his share of a joke.

"I was thinking of Mr. Finch," answered the accountant, "he is an oddity, if ever there was one, and his sister I think is odder still."

"Would she suit?" asked Mr. Bemmidge significantly.

"I do not know what she might have done thirty years ago," was the reply, "but she certainly would not now."

"That's a pity, but at any rate you seem to have been in luck's way," remarked the wine merchant; "I wish I could get such a chance."

"Perhaps you may, some day; and as I said before, there need be some profit, for there has been much loss. There's a confoundedly annoying thing to find lying for one," he added, picking up a letter, which he handed to Mr. Bemmidge, who first read it through attentively, and then agreed that it was annoying.

"If they begin to make objections about discounting," proceeded Mr. Geith, "I must shift my

account, for it would play the deuce with me to
have to refuse bills, and I must refuse them if I
cannot get them passed to my credit before they
are due.   With an extending business too, like
mine, the matter becomes very serious indeed."

"London bankers are Herods," said Mr. Bemmidge; "they strangle all the young businesses
they can lay their hands on.   The fact is, that in
another generation or two, there will be no small
traders at all.   Every business will belong to a
millionaire or a company, and men like ourselves
will have to be clerks or porters."

"It will be a bad day for England," observed
George, "when she sees the last of her middle
men."   And he felt desperately democratical as he
spoke.

"You would think," went on Mr. Bemmidge,
"that the bankers here were sworn together to
prevent an honest, struggling man rising.   There
was a merchant in the office the other day, from
Ireland, and he asked me what the London banks
were established for.

"I told him I did not know, unless it was to
help the rich to rob the poor. "What do you think
they are for?" said I.

"'Faith, and I don't know,' said he, 'for the devil another thing can I see that they keep open for, except to have crossed cheques paid through them.'"

"And he was right," observed George Geith, sulkily, "they won't discount; they won't advance. I had a cheque returned to me in the spring with N.S. on it, when I was only two pounds short, and had paid in the day before, a couple of hundreds in post bills and country orders."

"What a shame!" remarked Mr. Bemmidge.

"It was a shame," agreed Mr. Geith, "and it might have done me no end of harm had it happened with anybody else than the person it did. I will do the manager the justice to say he apologized, and said if he had known about the post bills he would have had them placed to my credit; but then, as I told him, a bank that is so infernally strict, ought to have people in it who know everything; and that if their particularity had damaged me, his regret would not have done much good. Keep a balance, indeed! not if I know it. I can employ my capital to a vast deal more advantage in my business than by keeping it shut up in their bank; besides, they would not discount beyond the balance kept, and I might, therefore, just as well cash my own bills, and pocket the discount."

And George, who was by this time very hot and angry, flung down one of the windows with a bang.

"If you like to change your bank, and keep a balance, I can tell you a place where they will discount good paper to any amount," said Mr. Bemmidge. "Nortons, in Size Lane. They are old-fashioned people, and have an old-fashioned connection; but if you want a really comfortable, respectable bank, you could not beat Nortons' in London: I banked there as long as I could keep a balance, and old Mr. Norton is a man you can go and talk to like a father."

Here was a prospect! One which in this busy world of London is not often presented before a man! To have any person to whom one could go and talk to like a father was wonderful; but for that individual to be a banker took away George's breath, and he answered somewhat incredulously that for his part he could never look upon a banker as anything but his natural enemy.

"Oh! yes you could, if you saw Mr. Norton," returned the wine merchant, calmly; "he is a perfect gentleman of the old school, you would be charmed with him,"

" I might, but I am very doubtful," said George ; " what balance do they require you to keep?"

" Five hundred." At which intelligence Mr. Geith uttered an exclamation of dismay.

" Well, you know it is the usual thing," remarked Mr. Bemmidge, "and then it don't matter how much paper you put in, so long as it is good, and to bank with Nortons' is in itself a letter of credit to City people; I only wish I could get back to them," sighed the wine merchant, and knowing the state of his pass-book, his friend could well believe his assertion.

" And if one wanted to open an account there, how are they to be got at?" asked Mr. Geith, " for I know I had trouble enough before I was privileged to draw cheques on the Merchant's and Tradesman's. It is almost as hard to get into a bank as what it is to compass the Kingdom of Heaven," and George began beating a tattoo on his desk, a sure sign with him of increased anger and impatience.

" I'll introduce you, if you like," said Mr. Bemmidge ; "although I don't bank there, Norton still speaks to me in the street."

"What condescension," remarked the accountant.

"Well, you know, Geith, it is thought condescension in London for a banker to do anything of the kind; and he and I used to be very good friends; and I know he will take my word for your respectability, though I am only in a small way; so, if you make up your mind to close with the Merchant's and Tradesman's, I'll go down with you any time you like to Size Lane, and tell Mr. Norton who and what you are. I suppose I need not say that Nortons' is a respectable bank."

"Indeed, you need not, I know Nortons are tip-top people, my gentry clients' cheques are as often drawn on them as on Coutts, and if you can go down with me now, we will settle the matter at once."

"But about the balance, Geith?" suggested the wine merchant timidly.

"I happen to have six hundred, which was paid to me since I came in, and I take the funds being provided as a sign I am to change my bankers."

"What a business you must be doing," remarked poor Mr. Bemmidge, whose mouth watered at sight of the cheque.

"Yes, I am doing pretty well, considering,"

answered the accountant, as he changed his coat and brushed his hat preparatory to sallying forth.

The six hundred was trust-money, which might be needed any day, but George did not think it necessary to tell Mr. Bemmidge everything; indeed, it was part of the man's nature to keep silence. Even from the friend of his heart and the wife of his bosom, had he possessed either, he must have withheld a full and free confidence. In this respect he was the making of a true man of business before he ever entered trade; and business, and long years of loneliness, and the constant habit of reserve, had all tended to make George Geith as uncommunicative a man, I mean with regard to his own affairs, as need have been looked for in the length and breadth of London.

His was a singular kind of reserve, however, being of an exceedingly annoying and deceptive nature.

There are some people who are, one knows, keeping things back, telling nothing, constantly putting their thoughts, plans, wishes, hopes, fears, under lock and key; and for these individuals one is prepared and willing to let them go on their own way till the end of the chapter. There are others again, who, though sealed books to most, are perfectly frank and unreserved towards a few; who can tell a story, if they commence to tell it at all, straight through without any lie, or mental reservation; whilst a third class appear to be candid, and yet are always hiding away. something from their nearest and dearest.

Like Ananias and Sapphira—making the comparison with all reverence—they profess to be giving all whilst they keep back a part; they play with everything which is holiest and purest in humanity, with its sympathies, its trust, its yearning for perfect confidence; and because George Geith did this, because, whilst making believe to bestow, he was secretly withholding, I call his peculiarity a sin; this phase of his character, detestable.

From a business point of view, perhaps it was a light thing to pass off as his own six hundred pounds, one penny of which did not belong to him.

It might be a venial fault in that instance, but George carried the same thing with him into every circumstance of his life, and was false about trifles when he might just as easily have been true.

He was not particular about the genuineness of his excuses when excuses were needed; he did not

care about a gloss being false, provided it served
his purpose; and accordingly he felt no prickings
of conscience as he put on his coat and brushed
his hat, about having implied an untruth to Mr.
Bemmidge.

The money was his· *pro tem.*, and he would
take advantage of having it, to transfer his account
to another bank, where he could soon get sufficient
paper "melted"—to borrow an expression from
Mr. Foss—to set him square.

"Nothing venture, nothing have," had for long
been George Geith's motto; and yet he was not
rash. He was not even speculative. He never
threw down his stakes on the chance of a particular
colour turning up; rather, he had the cards, and
played them boldly and rapidly.

To keep the business ball constantly moving had
been his aim for years; and to be thwarted in
this laudable endeavour by the perverseness of a
banker was more than his temper could bear.

"An honest tradesman," he remarked to Mr.
Bemmidge, "has to be content to see his two or
two and a half per cent.; but whom these banks
rob to pay the dividends they do, is a mystery to
me. I should like to have the overhauling of

some of their books; I wonder what holes I should
be able to pick out in them." And so he fumed
and fretted whilst the pair walked along Fen-
church Street, and thence to the Merchant's and
Tradesman's, where George paid the six hundred
in with a certain of triumph and sense of victory.

Afterwards, he accompanied Mr. Bemmidge to
Size Lane, in which cheerful locality Nortons'
bank had been established for upwards of a cen-
tury.

Externally, the bank was dingy; internally, it
was dirty. Further, it was dark, small and un-
imposing. At the Merchant's and Tradesman's all
was plate glass, frescoes, mouldings, handsome
flooring, elaborate ceilings. Behind counters, the
highly-polished mahogany whereof shone like a
mirror, were ranged rows of clerks, who made themselves as generally disagreeable as it was in the
power of bank clerks to do; and in remoter
regions, separated by glazed partitions from the
vulgar herd, was the sanctum of the manager
—a gentleman who united the conciliating manners of a bear with the appearance of a fop.

In Size Lane, how different! Through a narrow
doorway the visitors squeezed themselves into the

bank, which was dark even in the summer-time, by reason of unclean windows, dingy walls, a pervading presence of green baize, and absence of even the most ordinary cleanliness. Spiders loved Size Lane; they spun their cobwebs undisturbed in the corners of Nortons' bank; they caught flies till their nets became such perfect sepulchres that they were forced to build fresh cities for themselves and families.

The dust of years lay thick on the shelves; ink, spilled by generations of clerks, stained the desks and floor. The once green baize, which covered the door leading off to Mr. Norton's private room, had faded to a yellowish brown; the short curtains, suspended from brass rods, that served to hide the three clerks from too curious observation, were of any colour but red; whilst the brass rods might well have passed for bronze.

It was generally understood about the establishment that the floor was scrubbed once a week; but if this were so, the boards certainly proved ungrateful for the pains bestowed upon them.

Mr. Geith thought he had never set his foot in a dirtier place; but there was an air of money about it, an appearance of there being such plenty at the

owners' backs that they could afford to dispense
with the modern adjuncts of decent furniture, cleanliness, and light, which went far to impress the
accountant in favour of his new bankers.

We are all a little apt to think that where there
is much glitter there can be no gold, that the more
ragged the miser's dress the larger and deeper must
be his money-chests. Though he had seen enough
of life, one would have thought, to get rid of these
prejudices, George Geith was still swayed by them,
and entered Mr. Norton's reception-room in a contented state of mind.

Somewhat awkwardly Mr. Bemmidge performed
the ceremony of introduction, and then retired
into total silence, leaving his friend to talk to
Mr. Norton as he might to a father, if he could.

Which he could not. Spite of the man's suavity,
his courtesy, his pleasure at seeing them, his interesting remarks on the weather, and his readiness
to receive him as a client, the accountant did not
like Mr. Norton.

" He makes my flesh creep," he remarked to
Mr. Bemmidge as they got out once again into the
sunshine. " Good heavens! did you hear with
what *goût* he gave the account of that poor fellow's

arrest? I declare, when he laid his hand on my shoulder, I felt inclined to get up and fight him. He's a hypocrite, Bemmidge; I'm sure he is. Spite of all his nonsense about their consideration for the father, and pity for the son, he had not an atom of compassion for either of them. Why could he not have paid the money, and hushed up the matter? The old scoundrel, he could well have afforded it, I'll be bound."

"It was confoundedly sharp practice," said Mr. Bemmidge, with a troubled face. "Mr. Geith, I knew that young fellow once; he was as nice a lad as you would wish to see; and the father is a very respectable man, doing a good small trade in the Borough."

"I think I shall go and hear the trial;" and as he wended his way back to Fen Court, George, after parting from his friend, went over all the circumstances of the interview, and found that the more he thought about Mr. Norton, the less he liked him.

The banker was a man of about the middle height, but so thin and wiry and erect, that he looked considerably taller than was actually the case. He had a long nose, thin lips, clear blue eyes, that looked a person through and through, and the quietest, most conciliating manners that ever a man made capital out of.

He was an individual whose affability might easily win the heart of a stranger in an inferior station, and whose quiet respect would suit people of a rank equal or superior to his own.

" Any relation to the Great Snareham Geiths," he had paused to ask, when George, at his request, repeated the name; and to this question the accountant replied in the affirmative.

" We have had some business with the next presumptive heir, Mr. Arthur Geith," remarked the banker, " or perhaps I ought to say, with Mrs. Arthur Geith. There are not many of the original family left now, I believe. There was once a clergyman ?"

George believed there was.

" Do you know if anything has been heard of him lately ?"

The accountant was afraid there had not; and, as he said this, he and the banker looked hard at one another, and came to an understanding on the spot.

" What took me there? was it chance, or was it fate? or do our lives move in circles, which bring us ever round and round to the same point again ? Am I, after all these years, returning to my family, and to people who know them ? Will that old man go and say that I was a clergyman, that I am an accountant ? Will he go and wonder why I left the Church, and talk on the subject before my face ?" And moved by the old strong agony, an agony which he thought he should never have had to encounter more, George covered his face with his hands, and looked back over the toil of years, out of the independence of the present to the past which had held so much misery for him.

Then humbly, and with a changed expression from that his features had borne when he went out, he thanked God that his enemy, his relentless enemy was dead ; that no untiring feet were searching him out ; that he lived now in no dread of one who might be following behind him, waiting to lay hand on his shoulder, and make his flesh creep.

CHAPTER X.

DAY DREAMS.

IT was some days before George Geith was able completely to shake off the disagreeable recollections which his interview with the banker had revived.

For so long a time he had forgotten the past, that to have it suddenly reproduced before him was like waking from calm sleep and pleasant dreams to the memory of some grievous trouble which has been forgotten during slumber.

In the happiness of a recent present, the past of long ago, with its temptations, which he had not resisted; with its allurements, which had successfully enticed him; with its sorrows, which he had not encountered manfully; with its shame, which he dreaded to face, had all gone down among those dead memories which we are forced to entomb in our hearts.

He had hidden their sepulchres away even from his own sight. He had hung roses and garlands over them, and forgotten there were graves below. He had strewed flowers, fresh flowers, gathered for him by the hands of the living, over the bodies he had coffined. He had looked out over a new existence, and found it to be very lovely; and behold! just as he was going out to greet it, there came a general resurrection, and the woes and griefs put aside, as he thought for ever, trooped back with ghastly faces to meet him on the threshold of a happier life.

Was it chance, accident, coincidence, or fate? he asked himself, as he thought over the matter calmly. Was it a warning? Pooh! what did he care if all the world knew he had been a clergyman; that he had forsaken the Church for very good and sufficient reasons?

Supposing those reasons were posted up on the Royal Exchange, what would be the harm? If the story of his boyish folly, which had entailed such an estate of labour and sorrow on his early manhood, could be suppressed, well and good; but if through any accident it was made public, why, well, and good still.

In fact, if people generally came once to understand that he had been a clergyman, he thought it would be better for them also to understand why he had relinquished his profession : but, after all, where was the necessity for him to be annoying himself by conjuring up possibilities? Who was going to tell anything about him? Who knew anything about him for certain? Was he not taking fright at shadows? starting at the rustling of straws?

If Mr. Norton did suspect, what then? Supposing he communicated his suspicion to Mrs. Arthur Geith, what then still? Sir Mark and Lady Geith knew of his whereabouts; what therefore could it signify whether or not all the other members of his family were made acquainted with it? Let the past go down into the deep; and George tied stones about its neck and flung it once again into the waters of oblivion.

The certain advantages of banking with Norton, of Size Lane, soon made him forget the unpleasant impression left on his mind by his first interview with the head of the firm. It was like a little capital to him, having his bills payable at such a first-class bank. Drawing his cheques on Norton gave him a certain standing amongst his clients; and though George knew it was all humbug; though he knew his bills would in reality have been just as good paper if Aldgate Pump had been written on them, he still was glad to be able to fall in with popular ideas, and endeavoured to humour popular prejudices to the fullest extent.

It occurs to me, at this point, that the reader may want to know what an accountant could possibly have to do with acceptances; why he should ever have required to make a bill of his own payable anywhere? To which inquiry I may safely answer that there is scarcely a business man in London the aim and object of whose life is not to get his acceptances into circulation.

Bills are to the trader precisely what notes are to the banker—pieces of paper which it is supposed represent a given amount of locked-up capital; and which enable him to do four times the business it would otherwise be possible for him to adventure, if he were always compelled to wait until his money was free—until he had cash in hand wherewith to purchase and to speculate.

Bills are the long credits business accords to her
favourite children, and indeed it is the abuse of
this privilege rather than its use which makes the
habitual practice of bill-issuing to stink in the
nostrils of prudent and honest men.

Ready money is best, they whisper; pay cash,
they entreat; and the advice would be excellent if
in London people ever had ready money; if they
ever had the cash wherewith to pay; if business
men had not always money locked up in goods
which it would be loss and ruin for them to
attempt to realize.

The danger of bills is, that men are tempted so
often to issue paper beyond the amount of their
actual capital; in which case, should the venture
in which they are engaged not turn out well,
bankruptcy inevitably follows. There was no fear
of George Geith falling into this error, however;
for if he did speculate a little outside his legiti-
mate business, he speculated warily. Up to the
time of his emancipation, he had steadily resisted
the allurements of possibilities. Let an under-
taking look ever so fair, he had passed on the other
side, and refused to touch it. He was afraid to
risk a sixpence on any venture, let it look as

promising as it would ; and, therefore, up to the time when you, my reader, first made his acquaintance, he had been simply and purely an accountant —nothing more.

Once free, however, once he had realized the fact that his earnings were his own, to do what he liked with, that he had no further need to lay by for a special object, for one sole end, he began to look about for secure investments, for safe speculation, whereby he might hasten the process of money-making, and add hundred to hundred with greater rapidity than had hitherto been the case.

The great evil of his own business he had found to be, its entire dependence on his own exertions. In it there was no casting of seed into the ground, and then leisure till the harvest; no sending forth of vessels, and idleness till their white sails re-appeared in the offing. Ill or well, if his business were to succeed, he must be at his post. Whether tired or not, he must still continue that weary reckoning up of columns, that never-ending addition, that constant calculation which in time wears out the strongest constitution, and weakens the perceptions of the clearest head. Even to himself, George Geith could not deny but that the

toil had told, that the business chains had worn
down into his flesh, and that but for his holiday
he might not have been able to continue at the
same pace the race with fortune which for years he
had been running.

For which reason he turned his attention towards
increasing his capital still more quickly, and, together with one of his clients, a man of experience
and high business standing, speculated in such
colonial products as seemed the safest venture
and promised the quickest returns.

And now the accountant began to do amazingly
well. In all businesses it is the first step which
costs. Once that step is made successfully, the
rest, to an energetic and sensible man, is easy; and
George Geith was both. Beyond all things he was
practical, for he had no visions of a great future
to be secured by any means, save that of hard and
unceasing work.

He did not speculate in order to sit down idle;
he merely did so to accelerate his progress upwards,
and to enable him to vary his occupation.

Figures! Sometimes now he grew dizzy after
he had been calculating for hours; and he knew
enough of man's physical constitution, and had

heard enough of evil resulting to others from inattention to such symptoms, to induce him to turn his thoughts to some business which should not tax his brain so much as did that of an accountant.

Merely as an accountant, however, he was doing remarkably well : clients trooped in, one after another. Mr. Finch was as good as his word, and Mr. Werne perhaps a little better; for both of which reasons George soon found himself rising into note.

From the moment that he began to bank at Nortons', fortune seemed never weary of showering prizes upon him. Everything he touched turned out prosperously. He made money, as Mr. Foss phrased it, "like dirt;" and, sitting in his office in Fen Court, looking out on the trees, the leaves of which were now brown and withering, it might be that some vision of future wealth, of a happy home, of a wife like Beryl Molozane, began to float vaguely before him.

Separated from her, fearful that in the time to come he should never again be domesticated in that dear old house, the same as he had been in the days that seemed so far, and far away, he began to understand that life without Beryl would to him be lifeless, that money would be valueless, that the future would be dark and barren; whilst, give him wealth and Beryl, a fair business, a pleasant country house—and the Queen on her throne would be less happy than the accountant of Fen Court.

A country house, like the Dower House, only nearer town; Beryl young, Beryl gay, Beryl something from which no man had the right to separate him; Beryl to greet him, Beryl to talk to him, Beryl to love him; good heavens, what a prospect! A home without sickness, without shadow, without anxiety; a home with a south aspect, into which the sun shone even in the winter; a home where flowers were always blooming, where there was no vulgarity, no shortness, no worrying about servants, no living beyond their means, no keeping up of appearances; nothing but peace, and joy, and comfort, and welcoming smiles and sunshine! Whenever George Geith laid down his pen, and looked out at the backs of the houses in Cullum Street, I think he did not see the gloomy walls that encircle the graveyard, but rather the Dower House, with its glory of roses, its wealth of beauty, and Beryl standing beside him in its old-fashioned garden, his for life!

Painted on the blackened walls, he beheld this picture; day by day, as money came in faster, as business kept on increasing, it grew more real to him.

Above the graves, behind the trees, he could see the glory of that ideal home; and he never thought—have pity on the dreamer!—that over tombs he should have to travel to find it; that weeping, scalding tears, stumbling over bones, groping among dust and ashes, he should in future years have to pass solitary through earth, looking for the rest to come!

Oh dreams! oh visions! oh fair illusions and enchanting hopes! does earth hold aught more mournful than the memory of your unfulfilled promises?

Sadder than dead children are they to our thoughts. Can we ever coffin and bury them?

Can we ever forget that these dream sons and daughters, for whom there is no resurrection, have been with us and are departed; that their dear faces have smiled upon us, and may return, to lighten the darkness of our onward path, no more.

CHAPTER XI.

ALTERNATIONS.

IT must not be imagined, that whilst George Geith was dreaming dreams and seeing visions, he neglected any part of his business; more particularly that portion of it which had connection with Mr. Molozane.

On the contrary, he worked assiduously, and made haste to thread the mazes of figures he had brought away from the Dower House, in order to put them into some sort of intelligible form in town. When he had accomplished this feat, it had been arranged he was to run down to Withefell again, and let Mr. Molozane know the best or the worst by word of mouth rather than by letter.

Having premised which fact, it is scarcely necessary for me to add that no grass grew under the accountant's feet whilst he cut and pruned Mr. Molozane's affairs into shape.

He had long known what the result must prove, and yet when all was finished, when the debit and credit lay before him, when the balance-sheet, in which there appeared no balance, was ready for presentation to his employer, George Geith hesitated and grew cowardly.

He would rather any hand but his had to strike the blow; any tongue beside his own to tell the poor, proud gentleman there was no hope, that the disease was past remedy, the cancer too deep for any surgeon's knife to cure.

It seemed so like ingratitude for him to announce inevitable ruin, for one who had been made so welcome, who had been so unutterably happy at the Dower House, to assure the owner he must leave it, and earn his own and his children's bread as best he might!

To sensitiveness, to over-delicacy in regard of others' feelings, George Geith could lay no claim; but he felt there would be something almost brutal in forcing such news on any man, and accordingly he laid by the papers when they were completed, and deferred making his communication, until a letter from Mr. Molozane left but one course open for him, which was to go to the Dower House and tell the man who had been kind to him, that the accounts were correct, and that he was—a beggar!

And as he arrived at this inevitable conclusion, the wind swept mournfully through the branches of the trees in the churchyard, and with sobs and moans stripped the withered leaves off the branches and strewed them on the graves.

Winter comes to all things created, that live long enough to feel its frosts. Snow veils the greenest fields, ice binds the clearest streams, the rain and the wind beat down the heads of the fairest flowers, and the leaves of June's roses lie rotting on the earth, when November fogs succeed to the summer sunshine.

Winter comes to all things earthly. It came and dwelt even in the gardens at the Dower House, and when George Geith went down into Hertfordshire again, he found that the leaves were off the trees, that the flowers were withered and gone, that the roads where the dust had lain thick were now deep in mud, and that the fields, wherein the first breath of a new life had touched his cheek, were sopping and soaking with wet.

Nevertheless, it was to the Dower House he was journeying, and even had the snow lain thick on the ground, had frost and ice chilled the blood in his veins, George Geith would not have cared, providing always each step he took, brought him nearer and nearer to the dear old home.

Where on his arrival he found no visitors stopping, and the same cordial welcome as ever for himself. Blazing fires in the rooms in lieu of the former sunshine without, closed windows and doors instead of the open-air life he remembered. What then? it was still home to George Geith; winter does not chill warm hearts, or change frank natures, and the Dower House in November held for this man of business the same rich treasures as it had contained in July.

And yet he could see a difference, not towards himself, but in the inmates. Miss Molozane seemed less at ease than formerly, Beryl a trifle graver, Louisa more womanly, Mr. Molozane—but here George's heart failed him, the man appeared to have a prevision of what was coming, and to have nerved himself to meet the worst. And what a worst it was! Looking from the warmth of the Dower House to the cold and damp without,

contrasting the calm of that sheltered haven with
the storms and tempests of the outer world, George
Geith felt that he might in one way just as well
have brought a warrant for execution in his hand
as the statement which confirmed all the worst
fears they had ever entertained, which virtually contained for Mr. Molozane notice of ejectment from
the last piece of ground he might ever call his.

But the truth had to be told, and after dinner,
when he and his host sat over their wine, he explained exactly how affairs stood, and proved that
the first call of the Sythlow Mines would bring
matters to a crisis. Laying his papers on the table
he pointed out the meaning of the different entries
to Mr. Molozane, who, after a moment's scrutiny,
pushed the documents aside, and then said, with a
weary sigh:

"It has turned out as I expected then, as I
feared," and he rose and walked up and down
the room once or twice, as though struggling with
an emotion which he did not wish George to wit-
ness.

He had expected, he had feared, but here was
certainty, and certainty is always harder to endure
than dread.

" What am I to do ?" he broke out at last, " where am I to go? what is to become of my girls? Oh! those cursed mines; if I had only the money now I vested in the shares, I could live, we could live here comfortably."

" You derive no income, no small income, I mean, from any other source?" asked the accountant.

" None ; you see exactly how I stand ; you know as much about my affairs as I do myself. Matilda will marry her cousin, so she is, I may say, provided for; but the other two have nothing, nor the chance of anything ;" and he sat down again and looked at the fire, whilst George held his peace.

" I must work, I suppose," began Mr. Molozane, after a pause; but who would have me? who would find any use for such a person as myself ? I might be an agent, or land-steward, or bailiff, to be sure. We could live on little—we have lived on little ; and, oh! my God, it is very hard that that little should be taken from us."

At which point the poor gentleman's voice broke; and, as the firelight shone on his face, George could see the big tears coursing one another down his cheeks.

" I must get Matilda married," he at length re-

sumed, "and then decide on some future course.
If it wasn't for the girls, I should not care. I could
bear it, if it was only myself;" and he seized the
papers with trembling hands, and began examining
the items once again eagerly.

"If one, knew what the calls would amount to,"
said George, merely by way of saying something.

"But we do not; and if we did, it could not
make any difference to me," answered Mr. Molozane. "No I must get Tilly married, and then
think—decide on what it will be best to do."

Was he wondering whether another daughter
might marry, and enable him to keep the Dower
House? George Geith marvelled. In a moment
the accountant ran over a list of possibilities, a
proposal, an acceptance, an arrangement of Mr.
Molozane's affairs, a grant of the Dower House to
that gentleman for life.

Could he blame the father and daughter if his
ideas turned out to be correct? Could he say
Beryl was wrong, or Mr. Molozane, or anyone?
Could he even, although he loved the girl himself,
wish her to do otherwise? for what could he give
her beyond a small competence? How could he
help either her father or Louisa? Wherein was he

superior to Mr. Werne, who could place Beryl high above all chance of want, who could make her mistress of the Molozanes' old property, who could smooth every after hour of her father's life, and give the girl herself wealth, position, comfort?

Could he blame her? With the death bells of his own happiness tolling in his ears, George Geith felt he could not; that it would be strange if Beryl did not marry Mr. Werne; and that the person who stepped in and tried to prevent her doing so, would have much to answer for, if he succeeded in his endeavour.

Looking alternately into the fire, and at the man who sat gazing hopelessly at the blaze, the accountant resolved to forget his own dreams, and to resign himself to a future which he believed inevitable.

From the days of Jephtha had not daughters been sacrificed for their parents? and should not the practice be followed at Molozane Park? Further, was it a sacrifice? If there were not much love, was there not an infinite quantity of respect? Did she care for anyone else? Could not Mr. Werne give her everything for which the heart of woman longs? Would not twelve months trans-

form Miss Beryl Molozane into a very contented
and charming Mrs. Werne? and if so, why not?
Let them marry and be happy, what did it signify
to him? Which rational questions he put to his
own heart just as Mr. Molozane suggested that
coffee was most probably ready.

"And, remember, Mr. Geith, I do not want the
girls to know anything of this," he said. "It will
be time enough for them to learn the worst when
the crash comes."

In an instant George was out at sea again. If
temporal salvation lay in Mr. Werne's hands, why
should Beryl not be taught to understand that
such was the case, and instructed to play her cards
accordingly? Or was it all acting?

For which suspicion the accountant hated himself next moment; hating himself still more when
he looked at Beryl's guileless face, which was
thinner than formerly, and paler, as he thought,
too.

"You have brought bad news," she said to Mr.
Geith, seizing a moment when it was possible to
speak without being overheard.

"I have brought no news of any kind," he
answered.

"You have brought then a confirmation of my fears—the Park must go."

"I cannot tell at all what Mr. Molozane may do."

"You treat me like a child—like a baby—like an idiot," she said impatiently, and left him in a pet.

Next morning, however, before his departure, she was at his side again, coaxing, entreating to be told exactly how matters stood.

"I shall hate you if you refuse," was the last shot she fired.

"Pray do not do that," he answered, sadly. "At any rate let us part friends, for it is just possible I may never see you again."

"Never see us again? Where are you going? To China—India—New Zealand?"

"No; I shall still be in London, but my work here is finished; and though I shall never forget the Dower House, it is unlikely that I shall ever have to visit it more."

"Why not?" asked Beryl; "Do you never go to see any one except on business?"

"Very rarely."

"And do you mean to say you would not come to see us?"

"I should like to come," he said, with a not unnatural hesitation; "but I should not like to intrude."

"Intrude! nonsense," exclaimed the young lady; "I know papa was going to ask you to be present at Tilly's marriage. He will want some Christian to talk to after it, unless Granny sends him out of his mind between this and that. I think I never did detest Granny so much as while she was here last; I had a bonfire when she left. Will you come to the wedding, Mr. Geith?"

"If I may—if I am asked."

"If you are asked," she repeated with a pout; "as if you were likely not to be asked. It is to be early in the year. Dick was of age a fortnight since, and Granny wanted the marriage to take place immediately; but papa said he should like us to spend one more Christmas together before she went."

Whereupon George began to wonder whether he should be invited to spend his Christmas at the Dower House, or whether he should have to pass it, as best he could, in Fen Court. Of Christmas at Holloway he had already had sufficient, and more than sufficient, but Christmas at the Dower House!

If they would but ask him, the invitation would make him happy through all the dull days of November, through all the dark, dreary days of December. Was it likely Mr. Molozane would say anything on the subject before he went away? or would he wait till nearer the time, and then write? Or would he never think about him at all?

"How I wish I knew for certain," thought the accountant; and the idea kept him in a fever all the time he was in the house—all the way to St. Margaret's, to which place Mr. Molozane accompanied him, and up almost to the moment the train was due.

"I intend," was the last sentence of his host, which George Geith subsequently remembered, "to put this matter totally aside for the present. Sufficient for the day—you know, Mr. Geith—and I fancy when my trouble does come, it will prove sufficient for me. Meantime, I will not make the present wretched, by looking forward into the future. I should like to spend one more happy Christmas in the old place; and if you have no better engagement, or if no better engagement should present itself to you, I hope you will join

our party.   We have not much to offer besides a
welcome, but that is at your service."

What the accountant said in reply, it would be
difficult for me to put on paper.   He only knew
himself afterwards, that he had accepted the invitation, and that the train which bore him back to
London at the funereal pace which trains on the
Eastern Counties line at that time affected, seemed
to him a fairy car floating far above all sublunary
carès and projects.

The man was hopelessly, senselessly, if you will,
in love; and the idea that Beryl was not lost to
him, that Beryl liked him, that Beryl's father
wished to have him staying iu his house, trans-
ported him into the seventh heaven of happiness,
and sent him back to town to work with redoubled
vigour; to serve a far more capricious and uncom-
fortable god than Mammon, before whom, but for
his acquaintance with Beryl Molozane, he would
still have been grovelling in the dust.

CHAPTER XII.

CHRISTMAS EVE.

IN the year of grace of which I am writing, Christmas came to every home in Britain in the garb which all Christmases, if they were properly minded, would don for the gratification of Englishmen and Englishwomen; crowned with holly, from amidst the polished leaves whereof shone scarlet berries; arrayed in frosted snow, which glittered and glistened in the light of the winter's sun; with icicles for his jewels; with white and glorious robes of state, Christmas, surrounded by his minstrels and singers, by his bards and story-tellers, by fair girls and happy children, by grey-beards and stalwart men, and smiling women, came sweeping through the City streets, and along country lanes, flinging largess as he travelled. Alms to the poor,

rest to the weary, mirth to the young, content-
ment to the old, comfort to the broken-hearted,
hope to the desponding. "In remembrance,"
Christmas fed the hungry, clothed the naked,
sheltered the homeless, visited the fatherless and
widows in their affliction, and beautified with his
beneficent hand care-worn and suffering faces.
Free from earthly mists; with the glories of his
radiant apparel, undimed by rain, unobscured by
gloom, Christmas arrived, bringing with it enchant-
ment to George Geith.

For weeks he had been working hard; early and
late he had been battling with balance-sheets,
schedules, ledgers, journals, cash-books and day-
books, battling and winning. He had earned his
rest. Even he acknowledged he deserved his holiday
as he locked his drawers, shut down his desk, closed
his safe, and began making his preparations for
departure.

Leisure earned, is sweeter by far than leisure
given, or leisure stolen; and the accountant, weary
though he might be, felt triumphantly, that, so
far as his worldly occupation went, he had not left
a thing undone which he ought to have done;
and that no memories of work neglected, of clients

dissatisfied, would disturb the holiday which he was about to enjoy.

Walking through the City streets, he seemed as though treading on air; he could have greeted every man he met like a brother; he entertained no contempt for the groups who were holding endless arguments as to what it would be best for them to buy for the morrow's dinner. There was a beauty to him in the prize meat, in the laurels and hollies that decorated the butchers' shops, in the decorations of the grocers' windows, in the long lines of turkeys, in the parti-coloured ribands that were tied round the necks of sucking pigs; there was a life in the scene he had never noticed before, a meaning in the merriment and excitement that pervades the streets of London on a Christmas Eve which he had never previously grasped.

During all the years he had passed in London, his mind had been like a broken instrument, out of tune and out of tone; and the consequence was, that no kind of human melody had been able to extract any answer from it, save silence, or at best a cracked and discordant response.

But now, the strings were replaced; and almost any hand that swept the chords was able to draw harmony out of them. Even Christmas, which had heretofore been a feast, which he should have liked to keep as a fast, seemed to him then the happiest day in all the year; and he could glance at the Christmas pictures, and read the advertisements of the Christmas stories without a sneer.

What a beauty he found likewise in the white country roads; what refreshment in the cold, crisp air; what quietness in the eyes of the bright shining stars; what exquisite loveliness in the laurels laden with frosted snow, in the great black trees whose branches were half-clothed with white! How picturesque Wattisbridge Church looked as he passed it by, lighted up, doubtless, for the finishing touches to be put to the decorations for the morrow; what a Christmas look the earth wore; what a happiness it was not to have to spend that evening and the morrow in lonely offices in town!

George was so wrapt up in bliss, that he had not sense enough left to whisper to himself that Beryl was the cause of the beauty, the refreshment, the quietness, the loveliness, the picturesqueness, the happiness. Doubtless, many philosophical men would have analyzed the enjoyment as though it had contained poison, would have taken away this ingredient and that, would have exhausted, evaporated everything save Beryl, and found that all else were mere accessories, that without Beryl all was barren; many might have done this, I say, but not George Geith. He was neither philosophical nor chemical as he crossed the threshold of the Dower House, and was greeted by Beryl in the hall.

"The horrid old woman is here," she said, with a comical grimace; "and you will find a room-full; when we had one affliction we thought we might as well have more, and they all look as if they were weary of their lives; and I am sure," she added, executing a *pas seul* on the door-mat, "I am weary of mine."

"Who is wearying you?" inquired George.

"Everybody; the drawing-room is a perfect Noah's ark filled with—you know what. Granny, and Dick, and Mr. Elsenham, Rev. Mr. Grey and his mamma, Rev. Mr. Green and his sister, Mr. Finch and ditto, Mr. Werne and his niece, Mr. Hastie and his wife, Mr. Brandron and his daughters, Mrs. Ponder and hers; and there is not a dancing soul amongst them, and we have been conversing rationally and making ourselves agreeable to Granny."

" You surely do not mean that you have been attempting anything of the kind ?" said George.

" I do ; I laid myself out to see whether I could not annoy Granny more by making myself pleasant than by making myself disagreeable, and I have succeeded to perfection. I have picked up her handkerchief, and handed her fan, and given her footstools, and got pillows for her back, and attended to her general comfort till I knew she was ready to swear. And can't she swear ; oh ! Mr. Geith, you should hear her to her maid; I would not be that maid for ten thousand pounds, for I should kill Granny, I know I should ; I have seen her box her ears for sticking a comb in wrongly. But now I must go to the horrors; you remember your old room, do you not ? I am so glad you have come." And with that Beryl vanished, leaving George Geith standing in a perfect flood of sunshine, steeped to the ears in happiness.

Beryl had included Mr. Werne amongst the bores ! Poor Mr. Werne ! rich George Geith ! to have such amazing confidences poured into his ears; to hear Beryl was glad to see him; to have such a home as this to come to; George verily believed he had entered Paradise, and he lingered a minute or two longer than he had need to have done over his dressing, just to make sure that he was not dreaming, that this happy Christmas eve was not all an illusion.

He had seen most of the people mentioned by Beryl on the occasion of previous visits, so that when he at last descended the stairs and entered the drawing-room, he did not feel like a man flung head foremost into a den of lions. He knew most of the gentlemen to speak to, and some of the ladies as well; and though Mrs. Elsenham evidently regarded his presence as an intrusion, she was the only person in the apartment who did not, after his or her best fashion, try to make the stranger welcome.

As forold Mr. Elsenham, who sat in a great easy-chair by the fire, he was rapturous if not maundering in his greeting. "How is my good friend?" he inquired, getting upon his lean legs as he spoke, and mumbling out the words as well as want of teeth would permit him; "How did you leave the City? he! he! Grand sight in the City on Christmas eve. Haven't seen the shops dressed this ten years. Sit down, sit down." And with shaking hands he forced the accountant into a chair beside him, and began rambling and chattering about the days, "when he was young and very different; when he liked the frost and the snow and the keen north wind; but I prefer the fire now, you see," he added, with a weak laugh; "I cannot get too near the heat; I'm old—I'm getting old."

"I intend you to dance Sir Roger de Coverley to-night, at any rate," said Beryl, leaning over the back of his chair. "I will have you for my partner; so remember, sir, you are engaged, and do not desert me for any one else, or I shall be very angry indeed."

"It is you that desert me, Miss Flirt," he protested. "You know you promised to marry me ten years ago, and you have never done so yet."

"But I will," answered Beryl, "if I can satisfy myself that it is lawful to marry one's grandfather's brother. I shall expect such settlements though, and lots of pin-money!"

"What a mercenary child it is, only listen to her!" tittered the octogenarian.

"I am only telling you what I shall expect, so that there may be no misapprehension afterwards," observed Beryl; and at this statement Mr. Elsenham laughed till he shed imbecile tears; which laughter so moved Mrs. Elsenham's indignation that she called Beryl over to her, and remarked:

" If you do not behave yourself with greater decorum, I shall speak to your papa."

" Gracious, grandma! you do not mean it, surely ?" said that incorrigible young lady. " What should you say to him ?"

" I should tell him you were flirting to a disgraceful extent with that Mr. Geith."

" It is of no use, grandma," said Beryl, solemnly. " Papa would not believe it. He knows I never flirt."

" Your manners are forward and unfeminine !"

" Some people like them," retorted her granddaughter.

" I shall certainly mention the matter to your papa," exclaimed Mrs. Elsenham.

" I will go and tell him you want him," said Beryl, meekly; and almost immediately afterwards she reappeared with Mr. Molozane, who asked his mother-in-law what he could do for her.

" I want you to put a stop to the disgraceful flirtation Beryl is carrying on with that man," said Mrs. Elsenham, from the corner of a sofa which she occupied in solitary state.

" On my word, papa," broke in Beryl, " I have not been flirting with anybody, nor speaking a sentence to a soul except to Mr. Elsenham. He wanted me to marry him, and I said I would do so at once if I could only make sure he was not within the prohibited degrees."

" Considering Mr. Werne is here," resumed Mrs. Elsenham, " it seems to *me* imprudent in the extreme. I do not know what you may think, Ambrose, but I feel sure Beryl will, to use a common expression, spoil her market."

" Do you really believe, then, Mr. Werne was going to bid for me ?" asked Beryl.

" I really believe, miss, that if you could behave yourself with ordinary propriety, he would propose at once."

" And then I should have a larger house than you, grandma ; and only think, perhaps six horses to my carriage !" exclaimed Beryl, rapturously. With which conciliating speech the young lady retired from the discussion, and repaired to the piano, where her sister was singing her sweetest and saddest.

" You are a perfect swan," whispered Beryl ; " do, like a good, dear Tilly, play something lively

and see if we cannot get these stupid owls to dance.
I am sick and tired of trying to talk to them, we
have exhausted every subject of conversation I can
think of; try a waltz, galop, anything," and thus
exhorted, Miss Molozane's white fingers began
rattling out "Labitzky's Aurora Walzer."

"I never hear that," said Beryl to Mr. Werne,
beside whom she chanced at the moment to find
herself, "without thinking of the commencement
of a story I once read; it began: 'Strauss was playing one of his most brilliant waltzes;' what happened
after that I forget, whether everybody was happy or
miserable I have not an idea, I only know Strauss
was playing, and that there was a grand Italian
ball-room, and terraces bordered with flowers, and
statues and draperies, and all sorts of pretty
things."

"You are very fond of dancing and gaiety," he
said, inquiringly.

"To be sure I am ; if I was a grand lady I think
I should be at a party every night of my life."

"I cannot think you would care to lead such a
butterfly existence."

"Indeed, I should; I can fancy nothing pleasanter
than to live in the sunshine and to die in the

shade," and Beryl was off again entreating this person and that to say she or he liked dancing, if merely a quadrille.

"For, I declare," added the young lady, "I must dance to-night, if only a minuet, with Mr. Elsenham.

"It would be very shabby if we were to leave you in the lurch like that, Miss Beryl," said Mr. Finch; "I can only say I'll do my best to prevent you having to perform alone."

"Really, Mr. Finch, you are a treasure," said Beryl, gratefully.

"And what am I?" asked Dick Elsenham. "I'll dance with half a dozen of them, if you like."

Thus Beryl got the party at last into motion, and I think, as a whole, when the evening was over, no one had any cause to regret that her exertions had been crowned with success. "Dance!" observed Mr. Richard Elsenham to Mr. Werne, "if you believe me, she'd dance till her eyebrows dropped off. Supposing she could have her own way, wouldn't she go a pace?"

Upon which comforting assurance Mr. Werne slept that night uneasily.

" I believed I have dragged that wheel," thought

Dick, complacently, and he was so well satisfied with the effect he had produced, that he danced with all the ugly partners Beryl implored him to select, and endeavoured to induce his grandmother to trip a measure with her brother-in-law.

Which suggestion proving too much for Beryl's sense of the ridiculous, she had to leave the room, just as Mr. Elsenham got upon his poor old legs and gallantly offered to lead the lady to her place, an offer she indignantly declined.

"My dancing days are over," she said, drawing a lace shawl around her ample shoulders, "and if you want my opinion, I should say yours are over too."

"Never mind, uncle, I will be your partner," cried Louisa in a high treble, "and I, and I, and I," exclaimed half a dozen girls, whom George Geith liked for their hearty frankness.

"No, indeed, Miss Loo," broke in Beryl at this juncture, re-entering the room; "uncle belongs to me; do you not, uncle? and he shall dance with nobody else."

"Unhappy man," remarked Louisa; but the observation was lost on her sister, who had Mr. Elsenham already in his place, and who looked as pleased as though she had just carried off a prize.

.. "Why haven't you got a mistletoe, Beryl," asked her partner in a pause in the dance; and the question wherewith he went maundering off to bed, led thither by his servant, was, " why haven't you got a mistletoe, Beryl? You could have got a good branch for half-a-crown at the greengrocer's in the next street."

"Poor uncle!" said Beryl, "he thinks he is living his old City life over again. Only imagine, Mr. Geith, what countless years must have passed since he was young. I hope—I hope—I pray," she added, almost passionately, "I shall never live to be like that, to be taken off to bed by a servant, and to be old, and foolish, and feeble, and doting. How much thinner he is; his legs are just like knitting needles; are not they?"

What, in the name of all that's wonderful was any wise individual to say to such a girl? Passion and ridicule, pity and amusement in the same breath! Each time he saw her, George Geith thought Beryl Molozane a greater puzzle; whether she was strong or weak, wise or frivolous, perfectly straightforward or a little false, the accountant could not decide. He only knew one thing for certain, viz., that whatever she might be, he loved her; and that for weal or for woe, in joy or in sorrow, he should still go on loving the girl for ever.

CHAPTER XIII.

DOMESTIC PERPLEXITIES.

OUR pleasures travel by express; our pains by parliamentary. Through the loveliest scenes the joy train of our lives rushes swiftly; at the pretty wayside stations we are able but to touch hands with cherished friends, and behold! we are off again; but if we have grief for our engine-driver, care for the stoker, how we creep along the lines, how we tarry in the rain; what leisure we have for surveying swampy ground, turnip fields soaking with wet; stations filled with steam and smoke, and snorting, puffing engines; what a length the weary journey seems; what an unendurable companion the trouble we are compelled to travel with proves.

Was there ever a long, happy day, I wonder,

even though it fell at midsummer? Did not the
sun hurry on his way, and set at noon, just as the
tide of our happiness was rising highest? Are not
twelve hours of bliss distilled into minutes? and
when the moment of parting comes, does it not
seem as though we had but that instant clasped
hands in joyous greeting.

With George Geith this was the case, at any
rate. Christmas-eve and Christmas-day were gone
almost before they came, and as he drove over
to St. Margaret's in the grey light of a winter's
morning, he cursed Time's rapid flight, and wished
that at the Dower House he could pluck all the
feathers from its wings; still, though the happiness
was gone, he could look back on it with unutterable satisfaction.

He had been on the enchanted island, and when
tossing in the midst of the ocean he could recall
its beauties. Though away from the sunshine, he
could remember its brightness; and, amidst all the
din and turmoil of his business life, he could still
find leisure to think of the Dower House, and the
happy quiet hours he had spent there.

Sometimes whilst waiting in another man's office,
sometimes in the loneliness of his own; now whilst

walking through the crowded streets, and again
when sitting silent in omnibus or train, George
Geith's thoughts hurried eagerly back to the little
green spot in the way he had travelled, and rested
there. That the memory of it kept him awake at
night I cannot say ; but I do know he thought of the
Dower House last thing before he closed his eyes,
and sometimes in his rare dreams revisited it.

And in sleep fancy played some strange tricks
with the accountant. Once he dreamt he was living at the Park, and Mr. Molozane was offering
Beryl to him ; and again, he was poor, and Beryl
was telling him not to mind, for she had plenty,
and she loved him. He was a clergyman once
more, and had come all the way from Morelands
to Wattisbridge to marry Cissy Hayles to his cousin
Sir Mark ; but when the bride arrived she proved
to be Beryl Molozane, who left Sir Mark, and declared she would have no one but George.

In his dreams he was an actor in scenes which
he could never have imagined when awake; and
by degrees those scenes grew real to him ; and
George Geith, sober man of business though he
was, came to believe that these visions might some
day prove realities.

For clearly Beryl did not care for Mr. Werne : and though it by no means followed that because she did not care for him, she did care for George Geith, still hope whispered flatteringly in the accountant's ear, that the girl might grow to love him as he loved her.

Day by day he mentally re-visited the Dower House, thought over the hours he had spent there, and recalled his Christams visit, the pleasantest and happiest of all; the walk to Wattisbridge with Mr. Molozane and Beryl, the sermon listened to from the family pew ; the old church wreathed and decorated with holly and evergreens; the gathering of friends and acquaintances in the porch ; the comical expression on Beryl's face, as her grandmother's carriage drove off with a bang and a crash and a rattle ; her little aside of " What would I take and be Tilly, to have to be boxed up in that hearse with Granny ;" the kindness, not to say affection, of Mr. Molozane's manner—a kindness far exceeding anything he had ever evinced towards Mr. Richard Elsenham ; the long, pleasant evening, which was all the more pleasant because, for some inscrutable reason, Mrs. Elsenham elected to spend it in her dressing-room, possibly because, as Beryl more than hinted, she had found the Christmas wine **very** strong; the gaiety, the laughter, the fun, the *abandon*, the life and cheerfulness of that family party; all these things stayed with George Geith, and rendered his existence a different one to what it **was** when my readers first made his acquaintance.

The Dower House was not closed to him. When he had finished his business there, he was not bowed to the doors, and sent out into the world a stranger. Rather the doors opened wider, and as a friend he could enter them more frequently than as an accountant he might ever have done.

He had told Mr. Molozane how isolated he was; how, without wife, mother, sister, or friend, he lived in the midst of the great City, and battled for his daily bread; and the result was an invitation to visit the Dower House whenever he could conveniently manage to do so.

"Whilst the Dower House is mine, I shall always be glad to see you," finished Mr. Molozane; and I suppose it is scarcely necessary for me to add that George Geith said he should always be glad to visit the speaker.

Meantime, it may be asked whether Mr. Molozane suspected that George cared for his second daughter. If he did, there can be no question about his desire that Beryl likewise should care for George, or he never would have thrown them together as he did. Like many another father, it is just possible that he looked upon Beryl's marriage as remote; that in consequence of looking afar off, he could not see what was just under his eyes; but it is more probable that vaguely and dimly he desired to have a strong, sensible, self-reliant man for his son-in-law; a man after his own heart; a man whom he liked, whom he had found out for himself, who would make his favourite child a good husband.

With regard to Mr. Werne, there could be no doubt but that Mr. Molozane saw he desired to marry Beryl; and there was equally no doubt but that whilst the father remained neutral, it was not a connection he desired. Before marriage, men are not so adaptable as women; they see something in the individual who comes a-wooing besides his face and his fortune; and, strange though it may sound, the personal likings and dislikings of the males of a woman's family towards one of their own sex, who desires to become one of them, are usually much stronger than those of the female portion of

the little community.   After marriage, male relations reconcile themselves to the inevitable with a
philosophy undreamed of by mothers and sisters;
but beforehand, they have their little predilections
and are as much prejudiced against this suitor, and
as much in favour of that, as women are reputed
to be.

It was thus, at any rate, with Mr. Molozane.
He had his pet prejudices—his especial fancies—
and he did not like Mr. Werne. He respected
him certainly, but no amount of respect will fill
the smallest measure of love; not that Mr. Werne
had any faults, unless being too good, too calm,
could be called heinous sins; but, simply, Mr. Molozane did not like him; and though Beryl might
marry the rich man if she chose, and keep the
Park in the family, and place herself high and dry
above the sea of want, still Mr. Molozane would
not aid in bringing about such a result.

Undeniably, he should be glad to see Beryl well
provided for, the mistress of a large establishment,
removed for ever from all chances of poverty, all
necessity for close economy; but he felt that if
Beryl married a man for whom he did not much
care, she would be somehow less his daughter, and

if the choice could be given him, he would prefer that her future place of residence should not be Molozane Park.

He and his had lost it. Let it go. He would rather it went away from him and from his absolutely, than that it should be recovered by his daughter.

It was easier to a man of his temperament to lose a kingdom and depart into exile, than thus to abdicate. If Beryl chose to marry Mr. Werne, well and good. Meanwhile he liked Mr. Geith, and asked him to his house.

As for Beryl, what with her housekeeping, the preparations for her sister's marriage, and the constant worry of her grandmother's presence, she had enough to do during the weeks following George Geith's visit, without troubling her little head about lovers at all.

" The puddings alone were," as she informed her sister, " enough to turn any person's hair grey ;" and when it is considered that Mrs. Elsenham was good enough to criticize every dish which came to table, and to inquire what had been provided for her servants' dinners, Beryl's trouble will not be considered imaginary.

"When Granny is not here, I could declare there are twenty different kinds of meat; but when she is here, they are reduced to beef and mutton."

"Mutton again!" went on Beryl, and at this point she made a loop in her chain and looked at imaginary dishes through this imaginary eyeglass; "'mutton again; I really wonder, Beryl, you are not ashamed to meet a sheep!' as if I could make new beasts to kill for her, the old epicure! I wonder which I hate most, her eyeglass or her spectacles," proceeded the young lady; "the eyeglass makes me shudder, but the spectacles make me long to do something desperate. The way she balances them on her fat fore-finger when she is lecturing me, drives me crazy. I wish she would break them, I do, and then she could not read to Mr. Elsenham. Poor man! I am often sorry for him."

"But cannot you somehow manage more variety?" asked Miss Molozane, turning her fine eyes on her sister, who answered:

"If you tell me, Tilly, how to do it, I shall be greatly obliged to you. To have to feed this garrison with our means is no light matter, without having to serve a table every day fit for a lord. If I could have 'the fish in the lake and the deer on the vale' from Molozane Park; if in this desert I could have the fleshpots of Egypt, and get something to change the manna and quails' diet, it would be different; but as it is, I must make the best of it. Would not Granny have made Moses weary of his life? would not she have entreated for the quails, and grumbled at them afterwards? I wonder if, when I am old, I shall care for what I eat and drink, and be greedy, and make myself disagreeable like Granny. I would not be in your shoes, Tilly, for any money you could offer me."

"Why cannot you have fish and fruit, and game and vegetables from the Park?" asked Miss Molozane, ignoring the latter part of her sister's sentence. "You know Mr. Werne would be only too glad to send everything he has down here."

"I know he would, but papa does not like it. He does not choose to have anybody's fish, flesh, and fowl coming here without paying for it; and he is quite right. We are not paupers yet, Miss Matilda."

"You ought to marry Mr. Werne, and then

these things would belong to you of right," said the beauty.

" If ever I do marry Mr. Werne, there is one thing you may be sure of," retorted Beryl, sharply, " that Granny shall never enter the Park gates." From which speech it will be seen that the idea of marrying Mr. Werne had entered the child's head, and was entertained by her.

" Bless me !" exclaimed Miss Molozane, and that young lady proceeded with her dressing.

" I think if ever I do marry Mr. Werne," continued her sister, brushing her hair vehemently as she spoke, " I shall marry him to spite Granny. I know nothing on earth would annoy her so much as to think I was richer than she ; and that good man is twice as rich. What a thing it is, Tilly, to consider what lots of money some people have !" And at this point Beryl sighed and looked over the Park, on which the snow was lying thick.

" I wish we had some of it," remarked Miss Molozane. " I wish Mr. Elsenham would leave us his fortune when he dies."

" I wish he would give it to us now," said Beryl. " He cannot enjoy it all, and he would miss nothing but the good books Granny reads to him; and if he likes them, which I do not believe, I am sure any curate would give him a couple of hours a day for fifty pounds a year. Any person like Mr. Elsenham, who has not a house, who gives no employment, who spends only about a tenth of his income, and lets the remainder accumulate, ought to be compelled to provide for young people like ourselves, who really could enjoy money."

"I suppose grandmamma will have it all," remarked Miss Molozane.

"Or Dick," answered her sister. "For your sake, I hope, Dick; for I must say I wish he had some fortune of his own. I should not like to be dependent on Granny for every morsel of bread I eat; and Granny will live until the millennium. Mark my words, Tilly, and see if she does not!"

But at this point Miss Molozane thought it best to change the conversation. Beryl had such a disagreeable knack of turning the worst side of her intended marriage out, of showing the excessive dearness of her bargain, that the beauty declined entering upon the subject whenever it was possible for her to avoid it; wherefore, on the present occasion, instead of replying to Beryl's remark, she commenced wondering when "papa would be back."

" Certainly to-morrow, I should say," promptly replied her sister, " or he never would have told Robert to take over the horses to Hatfield. What a long ride he will have of it, to be sure ! Had I been in his place, I should rather have gone into town, and come back by train to St. Margaret's."

" He cannot endure London," was all the remark Miss Molozane made.

" I wish Jane was better," groaned Beryl, reverting to housekeeping troubles. " It is so awkward having, as I may say, only one servant, and Robert away, and that fine lady and gentleman of Granny's to be waited on and cooked for ; if it were not for Louey I don't know how I should manage at all."

" Can you not get help from the village ?"

" By paying, Tilly, by paying ; and I have to consider every sixpence. I cannot worry papa for money, I cannot, cannot, cannot do it ;" and Beryl's cheeks grew red as she said this.

" I had a few sovereigns of my own," she resumed, " and they are gone, and Louey broke open her box and gave me all she had, thirty-five shillings, and that is gone, all gone, to give that old woman, who might just as well be at Wattisbridge Inn, dainties and tit-bits! It is no wonder I hate her."

"Oh! Beryl, I am so sorry," broke out the beauty. "If you had only asked me yesterday I could have given you ten pounds, but I have spent it; I had no idea you and Louey were using your own money, or I would have given it to you."

"I would not have had it," returned Beryl, snappishly, "for you get it from Granny, and I will not have her money; only, remember this, Tilly, that if you are going to be married at all, the sooner you are married and out of this the better I shall be pleased."

With which gracious speech, Miss Beryl, whose temper had been that day tried beyond its power of endurance, flounced out of the room to see if domestic matters were progressing to her satisfaction.

It was a wretched afternoon; the snow was lying thick on the roads, and the sky was dull and leaden and heavy; no walking could be had, though Beryl felt if she could but get out for an hour she might calm down her irritation, and be fitter for the task of entertaining her grandmother and Mr. Elsenham through the interminable evening. Dick was dressing to go out for dinner, and Beryl wished she was going too—"Or rather I wish," she corrected herself, "they were all going, and I to stay at home;" in default of which desire being gratified, she commenced roaming about the house seeking rest and finding none.

Because, wherever she went she encountered her grandmother, or something connected with her grandmother; met either that lady marching about holding herself like a soldier on parade, or the lady's-maid in the passages, or Mr. Elsenham's man on the staircase.

Finally, although the library was littered with various inferior articles belonging to the *trousseau* on which the Withefell dressmaker was spending her best skill, Beryl took up her position there, and sat looking out at the terrace, where they had all passed so many merry hours during the previous summer, till the afternoon darkened into twilight, and twilight deepened into night.

With candles came Mrs. Elsenham to inspect the needlewoman's progress through her eyeglass, and from her distant chair Beryl, whose vision was perfect, watched the proceedings, saw Mrs. Elsenham's stately airs of patronage, her wooden-smile of approbation, and heard the dressmaker's ma'am, ma'am, ma'am, repeated, till she could have anathematized the creature for her obsequiousness.

The town lady's one great aim was to impress the provincial sempstress with the honour she was conferring upon her by suffering the future Mrs. Elsenham's apparel to be made by any but a person living at the West-End. One might have thought, to hear her, that a handkerchief could not be properly hemmed except within a given distance of the parks; and that it was impossible for stitching to be passable a mile from Piccadilly. Nevertheless, Mrs. Elsenham was pleased finally to observe the work was very creditable, and the marking " beautiful." " I must really show it to Gibbs," said Mrs. Elsenham, referring to her maid, and actually ignoring the fact that her maid had seen the work and reported upon its quality to her mistress. With this gracious speech, Beryl's grandmother left the apartment, leaving a general effect of trailing black satin and sweeping black velvet behind her.

" What nonsense it all is," remarked Beryl, coming to the table and tossing over the laces and cambrics with no tender hand. " The only good

I can see in it, Miss Sparks, is that it has kept your fingers out of mischief, and will put money in your pocket. As for me, if ever I marry—if ever—I'll walk to church in a cotton morning gown and straw bonnet."

" Law, Miss Beryl, how you do talk, to be sure; what would any gentleman say to a lady dressed like that?"

" I am quite unable to tell you what he would say," answered Beryl, laughing: " I can only tell you what I would do. Supposing, now, I was engaged to-day, I should like to be married to-morrow; and have none of this fuss, and trouble, and worry, and expense."

" Well, it is an expense, miss, to be sure;" agreed the complaisant Miss Sparks: " but then, it is a thing that mostly comes only once in a life-time."

" It does not come once to some people," Beryl was just about to remark, when she luckily remembered that Miss Sparks had arrived at an age when her chance of changing her name was small; for which reason the young lady altered her sentence into—" Once is often enough; and if it involves all this trouble, it is, in my opinion, once too often."

"If it was your own, Miss Beryl, you would think differently."

"Perhaps I might," was the reply; "but, at any rate, that is what I think now;" and with this speech, Beryl wandered out of the room, to plunge into domestic troubles again, and to help as best she might to preserve order almost in the midst of chaos.

"The next time, Jane, that you upset a kettle of scalding water over yourself when Granny is here," she remarked to the cook who was laid up in consequence of having performed that feat, "I really shall be cross. As if you could not have chosen some better opportunity;" and thus scolding, Beryl nursed the woman and saw to her wants.

"I don't like to see you messing about, miss," pleaded the sufferer. "If I do need anything, Ann could come to me now and then."

"Ann has trouble enough of her own about the dinner, without attending to you," said Beryl, as she poured the poor soul out a cup of tea. "And now, don't fret, but make haste and get well, Jane; that is the wisest thing you can do."

After which philosophical remark, the young lady settled her patient down for a sleep, first as-

suring her that she had made the pastry herself;
"so I know it will be good, and Granny will eat till
she makes herself ill; and then she will take boxes
of blue pills to make herself worse."

So far as the eating was concerned, Beryl proved
a true prophet; for Mrs. Elsenham did full justice
to the tarts.

"If I were you," she said to Beryl, "I should
turn Ann in to cook, and get rid of Jane altogether.
Ann can send up a far better dinner than Jane.
That crust was delicious," and Mrs. Elsenham was
graciously pleased, on the strength of this assertion,
to take another glass of port, a wine she particularly
affected.

Whether it was the port, or the pastry, or the
entrées, Beryl did not know; but never before had
her grandmother been so gracious to her as on this
especial evening. She even asked Beryl to sing;
and was so kind as to remark—waking up from a
nap, be it observed—"that, although her voice had no
power, or variety, or flexibility, it was still sweet, a
soothing voice," finished Mrs. Elsenham; whereupon
her brother-in-law, jumping up from a distant sofa,
added, "Yes, that is precisely it, Maria; you have hit
it exactly; Beryl's singing always sends me to sleep."

" So that I am of some use in the world, if only as a sedative," replied Beryl ; adding, in a lower voice, to her sister, "just as Granny is an irritant."

" Sing something else," said the commander-in-chief.

" Yes, do, Beryl. Sing, 'I remember,' " echoed Mr. Elsenham ; and, in his cracked old voice, he hummed with her :

" I remember, I remember, how my childhood fleeted by;
All the snows of the December, all the warmth of the July."

'Till he had to break off, coughing violently, which brought down a scolding from Mrs. Elsenham, who assured him he ought to know better than to attempt to sing anything.

" It is all very well for young people," added his ample relative; " but it does not do for persons of our age to try to pass for nightingales."

" Goodness, grandmama, did you ever try to pass for one ?" asked Beryl, facing round on the music stool to put the question.

" Don't be pert, miss," was all the satisfaction she got from Mrs. Elsenham ; whilst the idea so tickled Mr. Elsenham, that he laughed till he coughed again, for which result Beryl, as it was her fault, came in for a lecture.

Nevertheless the evening passed off on the whole tranquilly; and the whole party sat up so late, that when Mr. Richard Elsenham returned home—as usual, not too sober—he found the whole farm-yard, as he phrased it, still astir.

"Don't move," he said, forcing Beryl back into her place. "Shing for—me—nothing out of your con—foun—ded operas, but shomething jolly. We'll shing 'Buffalo gals' together. Matilda, you keep away; we don't want you; do we, Beryl?"

"Richard, I am ashamed of you," said Mrs. Elsenham, severely.

"Why," he asked, steadying himself against the piano.

"To see you come home in such a disgraceful condition! Go to bed at once!"

"That is what you do, old lady, I suppose," he retorted; and to cut short the controversy, which would soon have become a quarrel, Beryl was forced to interpose, and escort her cousin to the door, where he turned, and with drunken gravity assured all whom it might concern, that "Beryl was a trump, that he loved her, and that his grandmother was a tough old hen."

After this, Mrs. Elsenham thought it time to separate for the night.

"I second that proposal," said Beryl, with a yawn.

"So do I, if it is of any use," added Louisa.

"Bless my heart, I thought I was in bed," exclaimed Mr. Elsenham, rubbing his eyes. "I am very glad to be awake, though," he went on. "I dreamt I was a clerk again at Martir's, and could not get my columns to agree, and he was raging about the office just as he used to do. Thank you, my dear," and the old man, putting one hand on Beryl's shoulder, shambled up the staircase, rambling on about Martir's and his balance, and how glad he was to wake, till his servant took him in charge, and left Beryl free to go to her own room.

"What in the world is the matter?" asked Louisa, as her sister broke out crying—crying almost hysterically.

"I am tired, Loo; and I am worried; and hearing that old man talking about his young days, and thanking God that he had waked to find himself the feeble, purposeless, decrepid creature he is, poured the last drop in my cup. I know I am expressing myself badly, Loo, but you will understand what I mean."

Which Miss Loo proved she did, by at once, after the fashion of young authors, sitting down, and putting the whole affair into poetry.

"Do not ask me to listen to it," said Beryl, sleepily. "Your notions could not be like mine, and, at any rate, I have cried as much as I want to cry; so good-night, and do make haste into bed, and put out the candle," injunctions Louisa obeyed after she had re-read her poem lovingly, and erased here, and added there.

"You really have torn yourself away from it at last," remarked Beryl, looking at her sister with half-closed eyes, and then she went fairly off into a sound sleep, from which, about three o'clock the next morning, she was awaked by a violent shake, and an awful apparition in an elaborate night-dress and flannel dressing-gown, saying to her, in a voice thick with fat and excitement, "Get up, Beryl! get up at once!"

CHAPTER XIV.

DEATH.

"I WOULD as soon have seen a ghost," said Beryl, when telling the story afterwards, and it may be doubted whether a ghost would have frightened the girl as much.

Never before had she beheld her grandmother in her undress uniform, and what with being awakened in the middle of the night in such a bustle, what with the glare of the candle, and the horror of what such a visit might betoken, Beryl was awake in a moment, and standing out in the middle of the room, asking what was amiss, whether anything had happened to her father.

"No; it was Mr. Elsenham," was the reply; and the words seemed to Beryl's fancy to wander off through the deep forest of her grandmother's cap frills. "He has had a fit of some kind, and a doctor must be sent for immediately."

"I suppose Walton can go," said Beryl, who had by this time ceased rubbing her eyes, and was dressing herself with all speed.

"Impossible; he cannot leave his master."

"Then Dick must," remarked Beryl.

"Cannot you send Ann?"

"Cannot you send Gibbs?" retorted Beryl; and the young girl and the old woman looked at each other.

"Ann is not able to walk to Wattisbridge," went on Beryl, "and if she were, she would be afraid."

"And it would be useless for me even to name such a thing to Gibbs."

"Dick can ride my pony," Beryl thought out loud; "I suppose he can manage without a saddle and——"

"Go and wake him at once," interrupted Mrs. Elsenham, "and tell him to start directly."

It was not an agreeable commission, but still Beryl started off to perform it. After hammering at the door in vain for a minute or two, she lost patience, and turning the handle, went in.

"Dick! Dick!" she cried. "Good gracious,

how he snores! Dick, do wake. (One might as well speak to a post.) Dick!" and at this point Beryl laid down her candlestick, and with both hands shook her cousin; an attention which he repaid by flinging both arms out of bed and striking her across the face with one of them.

"You are like a vicious horse," said Beryl, "that kicks if it is touched. Can you not waken enough to know who I am? I am Beryl, Dick.

"And what the' devil do you want with me?" was the courteous reply.

"I want you to get up; Mr. Elsenham is very ill, and we have nobody to send for a doctor, and you can ride my pony."

Whereupon Miss Molozane's *fiancé* cursed himself if he would do anything of the kind.

"But he has had a fit," remonstrated Beryl, "and it may kill him."

"Give him another chance for his life then, by keeping the doctor away," growled Dick, and he deliberately settled himself among the pillows for another sleep.

"You don't mean to say you will not get up?" cried Beryl aghast: "I am perfectly serious, Dick, we have not a soul about the place who can go but yourself, and Mr. Elsenham is in great danger."

To which the unselfish young man replied that he did not care a d—— if the doctor never came, that he would ride over in the morning, if she liked, but that he would not stir a foot then, no, not for the Queen, if she asked him.

"If it was worth my while I would make you get up, you great lazy, useless sot," gasped Beryl, in a rage, and she went out of the room banging the door after her, and ran to Mr. Elsenham's apartment to see what was really the matter.

"The doctor?" said Walton to her inquiringly.

"Has Dick gone?" asked Mrs. Elsenham.

"Not yet," answered Beryl.

"Good God!" exclaimed her grandmother, "he will be dead before we can get any help; tell him not to delay, and to ride fast."

"I want you, Tilly," was all Beryl said in answer to this, and seizing her sister by the arm, she hurried her away down-stairs, across the kitchen, along stone passages, and so finally out into the yard, talking to her as she went.

"Then who is to go, if Dick won't?" asked Miss Molozane.

" I will," answered Beryl; " I am not afraid of going, Trot will not be long cantering over, and I can come back with Dr. Mawley."

" You, Beryl?" said the beauty.

" Yes, I, Beryl, unless you will go in my place."

" What would papa say?"

" That no child of his should marry a man who lies in bed and lets women do men's work," returned Beryl, fiercely;" at least, I know if I were Mr. Molozane, that is what I should say."

" But, Beryl——"

" Shall we let Mr. Elsenham die, and not stretch out a finger to save him?" interrupted Beryl; " if that is what you would like I cannot do it, so hold me the lantern, Tilly, and make yourself of more use than your future husband."

Very mutely Miss Molozane obeyed this imperious command. If she disliked picking her steps across the wet yard she was afraid to say so; if she felt it horribly lonely to remain with Trot whilst Beryl ran back for her bonnet and shawl she yet never ventured to leave her post; if it went against the grain to see Beryl doing ostler's work, slipping on Trot's bridle and tightening his girths, she did not venture to remonstrate, for Beryl never let

her forget whose fault it was that forced her into
the stable and out into the night.

"I would not marry Dick," said Beryl, pulling
the straps till Trot groaned audibly, "I would not
marry Dick, if he were as rich as Rothschild, and a
duke into the bargain, I would rather marry Mr.
Elsenham; and if I was you," went on the excited
young lady, taking up the stirrup-leather a hole
as she spoke, "I would break off the match now,
even if you had to end your days in the workhouse.
I never felt so tempted in all my life as I did to
pour a jug of water over him; I wish you would
go back and do it for me, Tilly."

"I will ask grandmamma to insist on his getting
up, if you like," said Miss Molozane, meekly.

"You can do about that as you choose," answered
Beryl; "he will perhaps be dressed by the time I
come back."

"I wish you would not go," pleaded the elder
sister, "I am so wretched."

"And so am I—about your marrying Dick,"
retorted Beryl. "Come, Trot. Good-bye, Tilly,"
and the young lady was in the saddle and off
before Miss Molozane could offer another word of
remonstrance.

Meantime, in the house all was confusion; no one knew what to do, or what to get, or how to be silent. The sick-room was a perfect Babel, while Mrs. Elsenham was in such a state of despair as to suggest grave doubts whether Mr. Elsenham had made a will.

"If he should go off!" she cried, marching about the room in dishabille, perfectly regardless of the presence of Walton. "If we only knew what to do. Beryl, have you no books about medicine in the house? Is there no one we could send for Mr. Werne? Where is Beryl? What is she doing, away at such a time? Matilda, tell her to come here at once."

"Beryl has gone to Wattisbridge for Dr. Mawley," said Miss Molozane, drawing her grandmother aside; "Dick would not get up, so she went herself."

"Beryl—went—herself," repeated Mrs. Elsenham.

"Yes, but we need not let the servants know it," answered Miss Molozane, careful even at that moment of appearances; "and do not call Dick, grandmamma," she entreated, as Mrs. Elsenham hurried out of the room. "We had better not let

Dr. Mawley know he was in the house; it looks so bad; it really is a disgrace to us all."

"I do not care half so much about the look as I do about the fact," said Mrs. Elsenham, pausing, however, as she spoke; "the idea of his refusing to get up—the notion of Beryl starting off by herself. I declare," went on the old lady, doing justice for the first time to the grandchild she disliked—" I declare, in any trouble Beryl is worth twenty ordinary people; she has all her wits about her in a moment. She ought to have been a man," finished Mrs. Elsenham, regretfully; "I wish Beryl had been the boy instead of Dick."

Which wish suggested such a series of complicated relationships to Miss Molozane, that she felt herself incapable of making any comment on it, and the pair wandered back into the sick-room to watch, and wait, and long for the doctor, who came within the hour.

"She is staying with Mrs. Mawley," he explained to Miss Molozane, speaking about her sister; "I did not wait for my own gig to be got ready, but rode back on Miss Beryl's pony. No; there is no hope," he went on, in answer to a question concerning Mr. Elsenham. "He may linger a day or two, though I do not expect it, but the result will be the same. When persons get to his time of life, it is wick, not oil, that is wanting in the lamp— not oil."

"Will he ever be sensible again?" asked Mrs. Elsenham, who was crying quite naturally and unaffectedly at the doctor's statement.

"I fear not," was the reply; "but in case he have left any of his affairs unsettled it might be well to send for his lawyer, or indeed for any lawyer, if there be no change before morning. He might be in possession of his faculties for a short time before death, but I greatly question it—greatly question it."

This was a habit of Dr. Mawley's, to repeat some two or three words at the end of every sentence; but in the present case his repetition only confirmed Mrs. Elsenham's fears, and she wept copiously.

"I wish Beryl was back," she said; "she would be of such use. When will she be here, doctor?"

"Shortly, I think," was the reply. "My man was to drive her over; and I told him to lose no time in case of any medicine being required, so we may expect her almost immediately."

About half an hour afterwards Beryl made her

appearance, but when she arrived there was nothing more for any one to do, save sit down patiently and wait for the end, which came just as the sun was rising.

"I think," Beryl had said to her grandmother, "I can lay his head more comfortably," and she was lifting it for the purpose when the jaw fell, the eyes turned, and the last breath passed the old man's lips.

"Oh, doctor! oh, doctor!" cried the girl, but before the doctor could reach her she fell on the floor in a swoon.

"Caused by fright and exhaustion," said the man of medicine, coolly; and he carried her off to bed.

CHAPTER XV.

EAVESDROPPING.

WHEN Mr. Richard Elsenham heard of his relation's death, he made an observation to the effect, that, considering the length of time it had taken him to live, he had been in a remarkable hurry to die.

As a matter of course, the young man expressed himself strongly, using various forms of oath on the occasion, and indulging in a greater number of expletives than ordinary, but the above contains the sense of what he said, and it was all that could be got out of him by any one.

Words wasted were Mrs. Elsenham's remarks on her grandson's laziness and want of manliness. His comment on Beryl's ride for the doctor was "more fool she," and his whole behaviour became so perfectly independent, bearish, and unendurable, that long before the funeral everybody in the Dower House conjectured Mr. Elsenham had left no will, and that consequently Dick was a rich man.

"It is an ill wind that blows nobody good," said the sensitive heir, to Dr. Mawley; "I am sure I never expected such luck," and Dick, released at last from petticoat government, began to assert his rights.

Almost the first use he made of his new freedom was privately to propose to Beryl, who refused him with such a storm of reproaches, that Dick mockingly put both hands to his head, lest the tempest should blow it off.

"As you like," he said; adding, with his customary politeness, "but I am damnably mistaken if you do not live to repent your decision."

"And if I had my way," continued Beryl, "Tilly should not marry you either—no, not if we had to keep a school."

Which keeping a school, being Beryl's idea of the acme of human misery, would have left her with the best of the discussion; but that Dick said coolly he was not by any means certain he should marry Tilly at all.

" Well, then, you shall !" retorted Beryl, with charming inconsistency. Whereupon Mr. Richard Elsenham broke out into a roar of laughter, and told his cousin " her temper was delicious."

Nevertheless Dick was quite in earnest. He did want to marry Beryl, and he did not wish to marry Tilly; and when he and his grandmother returned to town, and left the Dower House to its customary quiet, it became a very grave question with Beryl whether her sister's engagement ought not to be broken off,

Pride urged one course, poverty suggested another.

" Unfortunately, Beryl," argued Mr. Molozane, " this marriage is the only desirable future I can see for Matilda. Suppose she gives him up, what then ?"

" Why, then she can live at home, like the rest of us," said Beryl, hotly.

" But will she be satisfied ? Without her visits to London, without Mrs. Elsenham's horses, without Mrs. Elsenham's presents, with no excitement or hope of change, will she be content ?"

" I am afraid she would be dull," sighed Beryl.

" And further," went on Mr. Molozane, " I really

think Matilda is fond of Dick, and that it would be a very serious trouble to her to have to give him up."

"To give what he can give her, up, I suppose you mean, papa?"

"No, Beryl, I do not. She had the chance of having much more than he can give her, and you remember she refused."

"I remember," groaned Beryl.

"And as for Matilda marrying a curate or doctor, or any struggling man, the thing is out of the question," went on Mr. Molozane, speaking his thoughts aloud. "She would be wretched with short means; no affection could reconcile her to a small house, untidy servants, and the want of society; you know that yourself, Beryl. Matilda must travel the matrimonial road in a carriage and pair; and as she likes Dick, I am afraid we must let matters remain as they are."

"But if he refuse to marry, papa?" Beryl asked.

"I cannot imagine an impossibility," said Mr. Molozane, coldly; and his daughter forbore to tell him her reason for thinking Dick might decline to fulfil his engagement.

Meantime the estate of the late Mr. Elsenham was discovered not to leave so large an available income as Dick could have desired. There was plenty of property, but it was property which did not yield a high per-centage; and altogether, by the time his various interviews with the lawyers came to an end, Mr. Richard Elsenham discovered, fortunately or unfortunately for Matilda, as the reader likes to take it, that it would be as well for him to keep on good terms with his grandmother, and marry the wife she had laid out for him.

Moreover, Dick had a very wholesome dread of Mr. Molozane. That gentleman, he knew, would have entertained no scruple about horsewhipping him had he jilted Matilda; so, after suggesting to Mrs. Elsenham that a settlement on his wife would be desirable, and carrying his point, Dick brought his mind to the starting-point again, and professed his readiness to run in the race matrimonial.

Mr. Molozane was anxious also that the marriage should no longer be delayed.

Drifting towards the sea, he was desirous that one daughter should be in safety before he reached it; and accordingly when the trees in Fen Court were putting out their pale green leaves, George

Geith, opening another highly glazed envelope, discovered that Matilda Molozane was, at last, Mrs. Richard Elsenham.

He had known previously that he should not be asked to be present, for the marriage was, in conquence of Mr. Elsenham's recent death, so strictly private that, excepting the groom's best man, there was not a single stranger invited.

" I never saw such a dismal affair," said Beryl to Mr. Geith, on the occasion of his next visit to the Dower House. " To commence with, it was a raw, cold morning, and we all looked blue. If you can fancy Matilda ugly, I should say she was ugly that day. Our teeth were chattering with the cold, and everything went wrong. The sexton had not the doors open, and we had to sit shivering in the carriages till he was sent for and brought the keys. Then he declared Dick told him eleven, instead of ten; and I believe Dick had, though it was all settled and written down, so that there might be no mistake. Dick and Mr. Harley Elsenham lounged in about ten minutes afterwards, and then the clergyman had to be brought from his breakfast, and came rushing into the vestry with his mouth full.

" After that the sexton put Mr. Harley Elsenham in the groom's place; and I believe if it had not been for me he would have been married to Tilly instead of Dick. Finally, I had such a piece of work to get off her glove—she always will wear them so tight; and Dick could not find the ring. He had put it amongst all his silver; and had to sort through about two pounds of shillings and sixpences before he could find it.

" When it came to the signing, Tilly put Elsenham instead of Molozane; and the clergyman was in such a rage I am sure he could have sworn. Just as if one was being married every day, and knew what to do by heart!

" We were very glad to get back to the fire, I can assure you; and I think both Tilly and Dick would rather have staid beside it than gone off."

" After the fuss and to-do beforehand," chimed in Louisa, " it seemed such a come-down to blue noses and three carriages. I never heard of such a shabby affair in my life. The house was turned inside out for months, and then when it came to the grand ceremonial everything, as Dick said, 'missed fire.' And if you believe me, Mr. Geith Granny took all the cake off with her, and did not leave me and Beryl even a crumb to dream on."

"She will be laid up for a week with it, at any rate, that's some comfort," remarked Beryl.

"And she will not be much here for the future, that is a greater comfort," added Louisa, as she betook herself to her writing, with the air of a philosopher whose territory has been encroached upon by the vain inhabitants of a frivolous world.

Poor Loo! in those days she was building edifices great and fair on paper, she was raising fairy palaces, and fought in ink with the giant Poverty, till out of her dreamland she routed the intruder, wounded and discomforted. With her pen she vanquished all difficulties, over tempest-tossed waters she floated into safe and pleasant harbours. To her age, to her hopefulness, to her genius, there seemed nothing impossible; and she said, over and over again, to Beryl that she felt certain as she was living, that if she could but be in London for three months, she should be able to sell all her manuscripts and make everything comfortable at home for ever after.

Mentally she asked and received fabulous prices.

Three novels a year, and as many plays, to say nothing of short poems and trifling tales, "things," said the young lady, "which I could write in half-an-hour;" was the work she thought she could get through easily.

"Surely," she observed to Beryl, "I could make a thousand a year, without any trouble at all, and you should copy for me, and we would get Miss Sparkes to do all our needlework. Would it not be nice, Beryl?"

"It would, only I do not think I should like copying," answered Beryl.

"Well, perhaps I might not require to copy after a little time. Oh! how I wish I could get to London. I do not mean to Granny's or Tilly's, but just to London, by myself; where I could do what I liked and say what I liked, without being snubbed at every turn."

Very far away seemed London in those days to the child. She did not know she was travelling as fast to the great city as the course of events could take her; she could not tell that before the summer glory had faded from the landscape she would have her wish, and be dropped into the turmoil of the modern Babylon, to make her way to fortune if she could.

Never came ruin much faster to man than it rushed on Mr. Molozane, and when the June roses were once more filling the gardens of the Dower House with beauty and perfume, Beryl came to understand that they not merely had to give up the Park but also everything else; the dear old home, the familiar haunts, the stately trees, the pleasant fields, and go forth into the world, shorn of riches and station, to earn their bread.

The news fell upon her like a thunderbolt. All her fears had never suggested anything to her so bad as this. She had dreaded having to sell the Park—having to live with the same straitened economy always; but to be left without a home at all, or the means to take another, to have either to work or to beg, had not come into her calculations, and for a time she moved about the house like one walking in a dream.

Such trouble as the two girls fell into about leaving the Dower House, George Geith, who was staying there for the last time, had never beheld. Such lingering walks over the pleasant fields, such tearful adieus to wood and dell, and fountain; such treasuring of wild flowers and ferns, and grass and mosses; such a clinging to the very earth, as

though it were in truth their mother; such sob-
bings and sadness, such long, long looks, that
seemed trying to appropriate the landscape to
themselves for ever; such silence in lieu of the
old mirth, such sick faint smiles, such flagging conversation. Never had George Geith been in a
house before which the presence of sorrow per-
vaded so entirely.

But that made no difference to him. In joy or
in grief, the accountant liked the Dower House
better than any other spot on the face of the earth.
He would rather have been with those girls in their
trouble, than in any palace in Europe; and so he
stayed on, day after day, stayed for the end, which
could not, he foresaw, now be far off.

He was free of the Dower House as though it had
been his own home. He could come and go as
business required, and always be certain of a hearty
welcome, of a reluctant good-bye. All matters were
talked over before him as though he were a son or
a brother. The irrevocable past, the probable
future, Mr. Molozane now spoke of freely to his
daughters, while George sat by listening in silence,
unless appealed to for advice or an opinion.

Worn out in mind and body, it often happened

that Mr. Molozane slept in the evening twilight; and then, quite as a matter of course, George walked on the terrace outside the library windows, either with the girls or with his cigar for company; and when he was alone one thought stole ever uppermost in his mind—would Beryl care enough for him in the days to come to marry him, and if so, should he ever have the means to marry her?

If he had been rich enough, he was by this time so sure of his own heart, that he would have decided the matter one way or other within the week; but George felt he was not yet rich enough, and he had laid it out in his own mind that he would never ask the girl to engage herself to him, unless he was prepared to marry her forthwith.

He would not have her pledge her faith to an uncertainty. He would work fettered by no chain himself. If ever God gave him wealth enough to enable him to marry Beryl Molozane, then with all his heart and soul and strength he would strive to win her for his wife. If not, why it was better for the girl to be free, for her to marry some one else, never suspecting who would have worked like a galley slave for her sake. Least of all would he strive by any means to win her now, when

wealth lay before her—when she had but to stretch
out her hand and take back the lands of her fore-
fathers, and be rich and prosperous, and happy.

Yes, happy; for with such a husband as Mr.
Werne, with such a sunny temper as her own, how
could Beryl be otherwise than happy? more espe-
cially—and at this point George sneered bitterly—
as she was certain that no such poverty would enter
the doors of Molozane Park as might tempt her love
to fly out by the window.

And when all was said and done, why did not
the girl marry Mr. Werne? Was it that he was prudent, or that she was shy? Where was the hitch?
Did Mr. Werne not know how the Molozanes were
situated? Had he no suspicion that the father
would have to become bankrupt, and the daughters
probably have to trust to their grandmother for
their support? Or had he proposed and been refused? George could not credit it; for Mr.
Werne's manner was not that of a rejected suitor;
and his visits to the Dower House were of almost
daily occurrence. Would he propose? would she
accept?

These were the pleasant questions George Geith
was wont to propound to himself in the evenings

when, sitting out on the terrace, he smoked in the twilight till Mr. Molozane joined him.

It was getting dark on one of these occasions; he had finished a couple of cigars, but still sat on, waiting for Mr. Molozane to waken, and for the moon to rise.

The bench he occupied was at the extreme end of the terrace, and close beside one of the windows of the library.

He had nothing to do but step through that window in order to banish his disagreeable reflections, but he preferred remaining where he was. At times George Geith liked thinking till he grew wretched, and on the evening in question he chanced to be in a self-tormenting mood.

Mr. Werne had been at the Dower House twice that day; beyond a doubt Mr. Molozane had communicated to him the state of his affairs; beyond a doubt likewise that revelation would hurry his proposal, and then, then would Beryl have him? Would Beryl go up and live at the Park, and become a great lady, courted, flattered, spoiled? Would he lose her for ever? Would the Beryl he had known pass away from the simplicity of her present life, away from the morning sunshine, and the roses heavy with dew, to become the stately mistress of Molozane Park? If she liked, she might do so, but he, George, would never wish to see her again; he would keep the Beryl he had known shrined in his heart, and spoil the effect of that portrait by the sight of none other.

He had just arrived at this point, when Beryl herself came into the library. Everything was so still around that George could hear her asking softly, "Are you asleep, papa?"

"No, Beryl;" and at the answer the accountant wondered if Mr. Molozane had been thinking his thoughts too in the darkness.

"I have come to ask you something," went on the girl, "I want to know, papa, whether or not you would like me to marry Mr. Werne?"

She spoke the words very slowly and distinctly; so slowly, indeed, that they seemed to fall down singly and separately into George Geith's heart, like pebbles dropped into a well.

"What should you like, my darling?" answered Mr. Molozane.

"It would give us back the Park, it would enable us to keep this house, we should not have to leave Withefell at all, it would pay our debts, and make us Molozanes once more," proceeded Beryl, without answering his question.

"It would not give me back the Park," answered her father, with a certain anguish in his voice; "it would not enable me to keep this house, I should have to leave Withefell in any case, for no man shall ever pay my debts for me, and nothing can ever make me a Molozane, with landed possessions and county influence, again."

"Do you mean, papa, that you would take nothing from Mr. Werne, that you would not let him help you, that even if I married him you would not continue to live on here?"

"I could not, Beryl," he replied; "I could starve, but I could not eat the bread of charity; I could work, but I could not live on the purchase-money of my own child. Leave me out of your calculations, Beryl. That I should be glad to see you placed beyond the reach of want I do not deny, but that your wealth should ever help my poverty is impossible."

"But, papa, from me, from Beryl;" George, holding his breath and listening as though he had been the meanest eavesdropper, knew that by this time she was on her knees, with her arms around

his neck and his hand drawn down on her shoulder:
" From me, from Beryl."

"It would not be from you, Beryl; it would be
from Mr. Werne."

"I think I shall marry him, and then you will
look at things differently," she said.

"Marry him if you like," replied Mr. Molozane,
"you have my full consent to do so; something
more than my consent, perhaps," he added, with a
sigh. "Could you be happy with him, Beryl? I
know he would strive to make you happy; but
could you make yourself so, my darling?"

"I could be happy anywhere," she said, "if you
were happy too;" and then there came a long
silence, during which George knew Beryl was
crying, ay, and perhaps her father too.

After that pause—"Papa," began the girl, "I
have to give Mr. Werne an answer, one way or
another, to-night: what shall it be?"

"What you like, Beryl; whichever way you
decide, I shall be satisfied."

"Decide for me, papa; say you will live on
here, that you will not leave Withefell; and I
shall then thankfully marry Mr. Werne."

Thankfully! with that sob in her voice. If

he could have got away from his position without letting them know he had heard the earlier part of the conversation, George Geith would have left his seat, for his own suspense was becoming so intolerable that he was afraid of losing his self-command. As it was:

"Beryl," answered Mr. Molozane, "I do not deny it would be a great relief to me if you married Mr. Werne from love, for he could give you every-thing I should like to see your husband possess, except family; and family in England, without money to back it up, is a mere empty word. Wherever I might be, whatever I might be doing, it would comfort me to think one child had a good husband, able to shelter her from all the storms of life; but if you do not love him, Beryl—do you love him? can you love him, my child—God for-give me for saying it, if it be a sin—my favourite child?"

"Papa, you will let him do something for you?" —she said this faintly, with her cheek resting against his. "If I marry him, you will live on here, where I can see you every day, and come to nurse you if you are sick; you will promise that?"

"My darling, if I stayed on here, I must starve."

"But if Mr. Werne——"

"Stop, Beryl, stop; should you like to see your father dependent for his daily bread on your husband's bounty? Should you care to see me eating the crumbs that fall from his table? Somehow it has pleased God to ordain that I shall be as Lazarus; but I would rather go away from Dives' door, and carry my poverty with me."

"Mr. Werne would be so happy, papa, to help us all."

"At present, doubtless," was the reply; "but he might tire hereafter; and if he did not tire, I should. No, Beryl, put me aside altogether; marry for yourself, if you marry at all. Consider whether you could be happy at the Park. Remember all Mr. Werne can give you; how fond he is of you; how good and honest and true he is, and then decide. Only remember that your decision can in no possible way affect my future."

"Louisa, papa——"

"Put us both out of the question, Beryl; if there were no such people as Louisa and myself in the world, would you marry Mr. Werne? If you would, marry him now; if you would not, do not marry him under any false idea of benefiting us."

"I like Mr. Werne very much," said Beryl, firmly.

"If you only like him, Beryl, you could never be happy as his wife."

"It is a great deal to cast aside, papa," she said, "wealth, and standing, and freedom from anxiety, but if you would not stay on here I should care for nothing; I should hate the Park with you away from it; I should detest living if you were struggling with poverty; I should be always wanting to get free again and follow you."

How would it end? George, in his excitement, rose up and listened eagerly for Mr. Molozane's next words, which urged Beryl to consider well before she cast aside wealth and standing from her.

With a pathos none the less touching because it was unconscious, Mr. Molozane told his daughter of the roughness of the road that lay before them, of the struggles they should have to make, of the poverty they should have to encounter. He spoke of the comfort it would be to him to know Beryl was suitably married. He said, that in the midst of all his troubles it would be a satisfaction to him to know she was high and dry above the reach of want; he told her precisely how he was situated, and what he proposed doing, and then he left it to herself to say whether she cared sufficiently for Mr. Werne to marry him. "For that, after all, is the only question we have to consider," added Mr. Mozolane, sorrowfully, " that is all."

" No, papa, that is not all," said Beryl ; "what I want to know is, whether you and Louey would stay on here? Whether you would have a share in my prosperity? Say yes, papa; say yes."

" I can't say yes, Beryl," he returned, " when I mean no."

" You mean you would not let Mr. Werne help you ?"

" Yes."

" Not under any circumstances ?"

" Not under any."

" You are quite sure, papa, you will not think differently at the end of six months?"

" I have thought about it for too many months not to know my own mind now, Beryl ; but you, my darling, you will not decide hastily? you will remember all Mr. Werne can give you, what a certainty of ease and competence you will have if you

marry him ; what a terrible uncertainty of everything except poverty your life will be if you refuse
his offer ? You will do nothing rash, Beryl ; you will
take time to consider ?"

"I have considered," answered the girl; "and
if you insist that I shall separate myself from you
and Louisa, that I shall act solely and entirely for
myself, I cannot hesitate a moment. I should have
valued Mr. Werne's wealth for your sake ; I should
have loved him for what he would have done for
you. I could have made up my mind to be happy,
and I should have been happy, but with you away
I should be miserable. I should repent my marriage
every hour in the day, and I should hate the place,
and the money, and the show that tempted me to
say yes."

"But you might feel differently in a year or two,
Beryl," he suggested.

"Should I ?" she said. "If you believe that,
papa, you know very little about me, though I am
your daughter."

"Besides," he went on, without regarding the
interruption, "you must marry some day, and
leave me."

"I never will," she said ; "I will never go so far

away that I cannot lay my hand on you at any time. You do not really want me to marry Mr. Werne; you are only trying me; say you are trying me, papa."

There was no answer; nothing but a silence which supplied the place of all words to George Geith; for he knew that Beryl had broken down at last, and was crying out her perplexities on her father's neck.

Never a silence proved more irksome than that to George Geith. Away in the east he could see the moon rising from behind a bank of clouds. If she once emerged from them, he should not be able to leave the terrace unnoticed; whilst, if he passed the window and descended into the garden by the steps, he feared he should excite observation.

Like most listeners, he found himself placed in a nice dilemma: to his right was a thick hedge of privet, to his left that inexorable window; whilst below was a trellis-work, just too high to jump, covered with climbing roses.

Nevertheless, George decided on leaping something; and accordingly, standing on the bench and placing his hand against the wall of the house, he vaulted over the privet hedge and alighted safely on the grass on the other side.

Keeping well under the shadow of the hedge, he walked quickly on, never stopping to draw breath till he was safe among the elms of the avenue leading to Molozane Park.

There he sat down to rest and to think. There were no regular seats along the avenue, but amongst the underwood there were the stumps of many old trees, and of one of these the accountant took possession, while he tried to remember every sentence of the conversation, to recall every varying tone of Beryl's voice.

She did not love Mr. Werne; she would not marry him. Her father would not let her sacrifice herself for him. These three facts came out of the conversation, and stood forth clear in George Geith's memory. Mixed with them was a vague wonder at the girl refusing such a chance. In its way it seemed to the accountant like a man declining to be made a king, and he marvelled at her. So astounding indeed did it seem to him, that he left his seat and went to look at the property she had refused, at Molozane Park, which, bathed in moonlight, he could see from the end of the elm avenue.

There lay the goodly lands that had been owned by the Molozanes for centuries; there were the broad pastures, and the noble trees, and the silvery lake, over which the eyes of each successive owner had looked; there was the great house, white in the moonlight, in which the Molozanes had found it so easy to accommodate guests. Back amongst the plantations lay the stables that the Molozanes had once filled with hacks and hunters. To the south sloped the gardens which the Molozanes had stocked with every rare fruit and flower. Never a miser had there been amongst them; never a Molozane but had been a prince in his hospitality, and royal in his expenditure. They had kept open house in the days when their prosperity was at its zenith. A few servants more or less, a few horses to spare, a more liberal table than was needful, what were these things, what were these mere trifles to the Molozanes, whose income was so regal, whose ideas were so kingly?

And so they had gone on spending, for each succeeding generation inherited the tastes, though not the income, of its predecessor; guests still came on; horses still filled the stables; costliest exotics composed the bouquets of the ladies who were always staying at the Park. There were carriages and servants, there was feasting and revelry; there was riding, and driving, and flirting all the day long; whilst ruin was stealing up to the house to oust the Molozanes—the liberal, open-hearted, proud Molozanes—from their beloved home.

Thus the years had passed, and from father to son, and from father to son the Park had descended, more encumbered, less valuable than of old.

Heiresses might have redeemed the Molozanes, but somehow these men, who wanted money so much, always married for love, or beauty, or grace; and the heiresses that fell in their way were none of them lovable, beautiful, nor graceful.

So long as the place could be kept up, the Molozanes still galloped on, and galloped down; till the property came to Ambrose Molozane, who married a woman whom all the world thought to be an heiress, but who brought nothing in her hand to help to restore the ancient family to its old position.

It was a very poor, shabby establishment, when contrasted with the establishments which had gone before him, that Ambrose Alfred Molozane kept up at the Park. His life had been a struggle with appearances, a fight with poverty, a war against circumstances, a series of useless endeavours to retrieve his position; which endeavours left him finally where George Geith, looking out over the old possessions, sorrowed to find him.

All the accountant's own pride of family rose up in rebellion against this man of ancient blood having to make way for one of the newly rich—for a man to whom the Park, with its thousand-and-one recollections, was a dwelling, nothing more. It was just; it is the world's discipline that he who has worked through the day shall rest in the evening, and that he who has not toiled in the spring and summer of his life must work when his manhood's prime is past and age is creeping on him; whilst it is God's unchanging law that the sins of the fathers are visited upon the children, and that for years of thoughtless extravagance, of lavish expenditure, of frivolity, and pleasure, and rioting, there shall come a terrible day of reckoning, when there shall be tears instead of laughter, sorrow in place of mirth.

It was just, but it was pitiful; standing there, gazing at all that was passing away from the Molozanes, there came swelling up in George Geith's heart all that longing for possession, all that

sympathy for the loss of possession which is so uni-
versal with man. Passing away from earth, there
is nothing we long to hold so much as earth. Land
is a visible wealth; green fields, swelling uplands,
fruitful valleys are to the most of us what out-
spread hoards of gold prove to the miser—tangible
evidences of wealth.

But the green fields, and the waving trees, and
the swelling uplands, and the silvery lake, were all
passing away from the Molozanes,—passing away
as fast as poverty could drag them. A few weeks
more, and the old place would fall into other
hands; strangers would be dwelling at the Dower
House. In the familiar rooms, new-comers would
assemble; where Beryl's feet had passed, other
steps would follow; where her voice had made
sweet ringing happy music, different tones would
enter discordantly. There might be laughing
children, there might be loving and wooing, but
there would be never again a Beryl in the Dower
House for ever.

For ever and for ever.

Could she cast it all away; could she tear herself from the old familiar haunts, from her birth-
place, from the home she had loved, as we never

love but one home on earth; could she do this? It seemed so small a matter to marry, so enormous an advantage to secure, that although George Geith had heard her say she would choose poverty with her family, to the Park without them, he could not realize that he had heard correctly—that he had heard her speak her determination, without a shadow of turning in her voice.

If she loved any one else, he could understand her decision; but for a girl whose fancy was free to throw away such a chance, seemed to George Geith incredible.

At the moment he never paused to ask himself whether *he* would wed for houses, and lands, and money, and position; whether he would not choose poverty and freedom, rather than wed without love. He only thought of Beryl and Molozane Park—thought and marvelled—until he finally worked himself round to the belief that she would marry Mr. Werne, and keep the property in the family.

He was wronging Beryl—wronging her for the last time.

Beside the roses, under the moonlight, Beryl was telling Mr. Werne, at that very instant, not without tears, for the girl's heart was sad both for him and for herself, that she had made up her mind, and that it was impossible she could become his wife.

She liked him better then than she had ever done before. She liked him for the way he pleaded his suit, for the intense love he could not help revealing, for the hopelessness of his hopeless passion, for his gentle tenderness, for his despairing grief.

What to him were then houses and lands? What were bankers' balances and a thriving business? What were the possessions of this world and the pleasures thereof to the successful man at that moment, when the girl told him she could not become his wife, that she could give him everything but love—but love, for want of which his heart was perishing?

Then, like one dying of thirst in the desert, to whom all goods and all treasures are offered, save water, he cried out in his anguish, showing her all his suffering, all his cruel disappointment.

"Could it never be?" he asked; "if he waited; if he had patience, would she not have him for his very love's sake? Might this future never come?"

And Beryl, blinded with tears, choking with sobs, had to pause before she could answer "never."

Never!—like a faint distant murmur it came stealing out of the lonely desolate future—a future which no woman's love might ever illumine for him, no fresh glory of hope ever lighten with even a momentary brightness. All the misery, all the regret, all the unutterable loneliness of an empty heart, was coming towards him, and "never" was the first faint sound which told of its approach. It was the sighing sough of the wind that announces a tempest, against which man must battle. It was the far-off grating of the wheel of the hearse which comes to take his dearest and best away from his sight. It was death to every plan, to every hope, to every joy; and in his agony Mr. Werne could not help exclaiming:

"Oh! Beryl, if it may never be; if we must part; I would to God I had never seen your face."

"Forgive me," she was crying helplessly by this time; crying among the roses, under the moonlight. "If I have ever made you think I could be your wife, if I have thought it myself, if I have ever done you a wrong, and led you to fancy things might be different, you know what made me do it.

Forgive me, though I shall never, never, never forgive myself."

God help him. He learnt at that moment just what his wealth had done for him—just what Beryl would have married him for, had she consented to become his wife; and he stood for a moment silent, with her hand clasped tightly in his, waiting till the pain should be overpast—till he could speak to her calmly and steadily as he wished.

" My child," he said at last—and, oh! how old he felt, and how young she seemed, as he called her by that name—"it is my life that I have lost this night; but I would not have you give me back my life at the price you imply. It is over now; the hope, the fear, the long suspense; and I can let you go, satisfied that you are right, that I was wrong."

But still he did not let her go. He only drew her nearer, closer to him, whispering, whilst he trembled violently, "Kiss me, Beryl—kiss me for once."

Had George Geith been eavesdropping then, even he would have forgiven them both. Some men do not find it so easy to coffin their dead hopes; some women cannot so readily help to pile the earth into the grave, as many think.

CHAPTER XVI.

IN LONDON.

IT was a hard matter for a man like Mr. Molozane to have to flee to Basinghall-street for refuge; and how hard he had found his trial to bear, was shown by hollow cheeks and grey hair, when he came forth from that sanctuary, free of debt indeed, but penniless.

The world was all before him; there was room enough in it to beg or starve; but if he wished to earn a living for himself and his daughters, he had no choice save to stay in London, where Mr. Werne obtained a situation for him in the great shipping-house of Murphy, Dowsett, and Raikes, at a salary of two hundred and fifty pounds per annum.

Mr. George Geith, who knew the rates at which the wealthy firm in question were in the habit of

paying their clerks, never believed in that two
hundred and fifty at all; he thought the fifty without the two hundred much more likely to be near
the mark, and the accountant was correct. The
salary was a matter of arrangement between Mr.
Raikes the managing partner and Mr. Werne, who
fancied that Mr. Molozane's business capabilities
were of the smallest, that, in fact, he would be only
useful, as he said frankly to Mr. Raikes, to be a
check on the junior clerks, and to answer civil
questions in a civil manner.

But in this Mr. Werne proved to be mistaken.

Mr. Molozane had no idea of taking his money
and doing as little as possible for it, and he put his
shoulder to the wheel in a manner which won for
him the cordial dislike of all the clerks in Messrs.
Murphy, Dowsett, and Raikes' employment.

To do nothing and be paid a salary for it, was
their idea of perfect happiness; to work before face
and idle when their employer's back was turned was
their conception of duty; and accordingly, the sight
of a middle-aged man setting himself to learn all the
ins and outs of the business with a will, being
punctual to his time, being honest in his occupation,
filled the young fry with unspeakable disgust.

But to their good or bad opinion Mr. Molozane was equally indifferent: by work, he and his had for the future to live, and though business was work he detested, though he disliked his employment, his position and his employers, he never slackened in his efforts, but laboured on for the sake of the young girls who were dependent on him.

At the top of the Caledonian Road, beyond the Cattle Market, there is still, I believe, a place called Stock Orchard Crescent, and there the Molozanes pitched their tent.

The house was of Beryl's finding, and I doubt if, all things considered, she could have found a better.

To be sure, even then the place had its drawbacks, but the situation was quiet, the houses were semi-detached, the rooms were large for London, and the rent not excessive.

Mr. Molozane could walk from thence to Leadenhall Street, and the girls could readily get into the country. Highgate was not far off, Hornsey and Crouch End were accessible; and all the new villas, terraces and streets, that now cover the Seven Sisters' Road, and the upper part of Holloway, were undreamed of.

Into her new home Beryl carried the same happy face, the same courageous heart, the same power of adaptation which had won George Geith's heart in the old days departed. She had wept out her tears; and in the spring time of life, as in the April of the year, sunshine follows cloud. Over Molozane Park, over the Dower House roses, over the familiar household goods that had been carried from before her face to strange and unfamiliar places, she had rained showers of sorrow; but the trouble was now gone and past; the pain had been endured and was over; and in the happiness of having her father with them again, in the busy little cares of housekeeping, in the occupation of making both ends of their income meet, Beryl, safe on land once more, forgot the fury of the storm she had breasted, and commenced extracting such pleasure as was possible from the new life in which she was just starting.

To a nature like Beryl's, if I may say so without detracting from any favourable opinion my readers may entertain of her, furnishing was a delicious employment, a charming amusement, which had not fallen to her lot previously. Even had she been compelled to cut and contrive, to grudge carpeting here and curtains there, shopping and ar-

ranging on the most limited scale, would have possessed the greatest fascination for her; but as it
was with money, absolute wealth, at her back, Beryl
revelled in upholstery, and walked about London as
happy as the mistress of ten thousand a year. Had
the girl known where the money really came from,
which filled her purse and paid for her various
little purchases, she would not, I think, have gone
on her errand with quite so light a heart; but she had
accepted the sum which furnished their new home,
and left besides something over for a rainy day, in
perfect good faith from her sister, Mrs. Richard
Elsenham, in whose hands Mr. Werne had placed
it before he went abroad, to try if there were any
balm in absence for a broken heart.

Matilda's honesty had been subjected to a severe
test by the trust Mr. Werne reposed in her. Her
necessities were many, her supplies scanty, and the
evil one had put so many pretty trinkets, heavenly
bonnets, and enticing dresses, in her way just about
the time the money was left with her, that she felt
if she had not hastened to place the whole amount
in Beryl's keeping, she never, never, never could
have resisted the temptations which beset her.

Further, Beryl's thanks were very trying to a

person who knew how little she merited them. Albeit a fashionable lady, a spendthrift, selfish woman, Matilda had a species of conscience which pricked her when Beryl burst into tears, and begging "Tilly's pardon for every hard thing she had ever before said or thought of her," declared "this money would make all the difference to them between wretchedness and happiness."

"We can take a house and furnish it, and get out of these miserable lodgings," went on the poor little thing, counting off all the blessings she saw looming in the future, on her fingers; "but, Tilly, are you sure you do not want it? I will only take half; I can manage nicely on half, and it is too much: you are too good and generous, my darling."

With her cheeks on fire, Mrs. Richard Elsenham implored her sister "not to mention it." She would, to do her justice, have liked nothing better than to tell her how small a share she had in the good work; but being bound to secresy, and knowing, moreover, the present would have made Beryl wretched, had she known the source whence it proceeded, she merely stated that the money had been given to her to do what she liked with, and that she liked beyond anything to see Beryl happy, and her father comfortable.

" I would give the world," she said, " to be able to be the blessing to anybody you have been, Beryl, and to have anybody love me as people love you ;" which was perfectly true.

During her interview with Mr. Werne, the beauty had thought that if such a man had loved her as he loved Beryl—such a man with such an income —she might have been a very happy woman.

As it was, Mrs. Richard Elsenham was not a happy woman, and Beryl left the house greatly delighted with the state of her finances, but sadly down-hearted concerning her sister's tears and mournful little speeches.

Then commenced house-hunting and house-furnishing ; what miles Beryl travelled ; what numbers of house-agents she consulted ; what scores of omnibuses she entered ; east, north, west, and south she travelled, to settle on Stock Orchard Crescent at last, to George Geith's dismay. Her chosen residence was too near the Bemmidges to please him. " He did not think Stock Orchard Crescent a nice place," he said, " and was certain that old-fashioned house at Hackney, with the

large garden, would have pleased Mr. Molozane far
better. For his part, he disliked Holloway intensely, and he could not imagine what the young
ladies saw in it to fancy. He advised Hackney. The
house was a better house, and the rent no higher."

But in this matter Beryl was firm. Louisa did
not care for Hackney ; she had seen that charming
locality on a wet day, and took up a prejudice
against it. The house looked dull ; the garden
damp ; the rooms were dark ; the kitchen wretched ;
there were no good pantries ; the situation was not
good. Louey was sure she could never exist in
that brick prison ; and, on the other hand, Louey
felt confident she should feel at home in an hour
in Stock Orchard Crescent.

"She has been amusing herself arranging how
all the furniture is to stand," finished Beryl ; and
George Geith knew that settled the matter.

The Autocrat of all the Russias might have issued
his edict in vain to Beryl, after Louey had spoken.

"Hang the precocious chit !" muttered the
accountant, as he walked away from their lodgings ;
but he spoke out of his anger, rather than out of
his heart. In the days to come he was glad to
remember Beryl had suffered her sister to choose

for them; he was glad to recollect every step of his wretched way had been determined on by others, rather than by himself.

After Whitecross Street, any home would have seemed delicious to Mr. Molozane; how much more the cheerful, pleasant home where Beryl, her sister, and one of their former servants were locate Something of Beryl's happy temperament must hav come to her from her father, for he sat down under the shadow of the fig-tree, which had grown for him in this strange land, contented and unrepining.

"Dare I murmur," he said, in answer to some involuntary expression of admiration from George Geith, "while so much is left me: health to work, and work to do, and children to work for? I thought at one time I never could have parted with the old place and lived, but we never know how much we can bear till we have borne it."

Listening to him, the accountant thought, that we also never know how much other people can bear, till we have seen them carrying their burden. He had wondered in the days gone by how Mr. Molozane would endure bankruptcy and beggary. He had pictured all kinds of possibilities, save always a situation in the city and a house at the

top of the Caledonian Road. The position was too
commonplace and comfortable for him to realize,
and so for a time George Geith felt Beryl's new
home to be a myth, and the increase of happiness
it brought to him incredible.

Never a man in London did the accountant envy
in those days after the Molozanes took possession
of their new house. He might have lived with
them had he liked to avail himself of Mr. Molozane's numerous invitations.

No more solitary evenings for the once lonely
man ; no more weary Sundays with endless pere-
grinations over stony-hearted streets. There was a
welcome always for him when he chose to go and
get it. He had a home, the door whereof was
always open to him. Let the day be never so dull
and weary, there was light and warmth waiting for
him at the top of the Caledonian Road, if he took
the trouble of walking thither for it.

He had not now to travel to Hertfordshire to
hear the music that charmed him most. Like the
chiming of sweet bells, the tones of Beryl's voice
rang in his ears continually. There was no more
winter for him, no more frost and snow. The
sunshine had travelled from the Dower House to

gladden his heart, and the man was so happy that his life seemed to be passed in fairyland.

As for Beryl, any one might have thought she had taken a new lease of enjoyment, that she had gained an inheritance instead of losing all she and hers had been proud and careful over, too proud and too careful, alas for them. There was no trace of sadness about her, no want of elasticity in her movements, no decrease of vivacity as she discharged her familiar household duties. If the past had worn any darksome channels in her heart, the glad, bright, full stream of youth, sparkling on its way, hid all traces of trouble away both from her own sight and that of her neighbours. It is when years have dried up the once-abundant waters of gladness, when there is no musical brook gliding onward to meet the future, when there is no green sward on the banks, no gushing spring of hope left to replenish the bed once filled to overflowing by the restless chattering river, that age, looking at the furrows worn in that bygone time, understands fully how much can be suffered by youth, which youth happily forgets to remember.

It was thus with Beryl, at any rate. Her troubles were dead and coffined, and she revisited not their graves. In some stratum of her nature each grief she had suffered was lying away hidden like a fossil; but like the fossil of an ancient world, were all past sorrows to the girl who lived in a perpetual sunshine, in an unchanging noon, where no shadow fell. Fond of the country as she had been, 'tis a truth which must be confessed, that Beryl liked London amazingly also. She had detested Kensington and her grandmother, but a house in London which held her father and sister, and unbounded personal liberty besides, was quite another affair.

Dare I confess that she delighted in the shops in Upper-street, that the crowds of people, the countless conveyances, and the eternal excitement, charmed her beyond description? London to her was a great theatre, with perpetually shifting scenes and actors.

It was a new world, containing a race of men hitherto undreamed of. The pace was so fast, it suited her active spirit; and she danced about the rooms of their new home, along the broad hall and up the staircase, with light feet and a lighter heart, in time to the strains of the barrel-organs that infested Stock Orchard Crescent on account of its reputed quietness.

In after days, when that house was again to let, George Geith went and paid the care-takers to allow him to go over the well-remembered rooms alone. Through every apartment he wandered, and at last returned to the drawing room, which he re-furnished and re-peopled out of the store-houses of memory.

To him it was bare and desolate no longer. In his fancy he saw her sitting before him, with the sunshine streaming on her hair; he heard the tones of her voice; he saw her bright, happy smile; he beheld the caressing hand stretched forth to touch Louey as she passed. Every picture hung in its wonted place; the very perfume of her favourite flowers seemed pervading the air; the remembered books and knick-knacks lay on the tables; and as he stood dreaming out his dream, an Italian organ-grinder struck up " Johnny Sands."

Many a time had he listened to Beryl lilting out that most absurd song* through the now deserted

---

* " There was a man, named Johnny Sands,
    Who married Betsy Hague,
  Although she brought him gold and lands,
    She proved a terrible plague.
                She proved a terrible plague.

house, but the strain provoked no answering smile from the lonely listener.

Ah, no! for as the air went ringing through the glad sunshine, all his dream melted away, and left him standing in the dismantled room—desolate!

" One day said he, ' I'll drown myself,
　　The river runs below;'
' Oh, do!' said she, ' you saucy elf,
　　I wished it long ago.'
　　　　　　　I wished it long ago.

" Said he, ' If on the brink I stand,
　　Will you run down the hill,
And push me in with all your might?'
　　Said she, ' My love I will.'
　　　　　　　Said she, ' My love, I will.'

" ' And lest that I should courage lack,
　　And try to save my life,
Pray tie my hands behind my back,'
　　' I will,' replied the wife.
　　　　　　　' I will,' replied the wife.

" Then down the hill his loving bride
　　She ran with all her force,
To push him in;—he stepped aside,
　　And she fell in, of course.
　　　　　　　And she fell in, of course.

" Splashing, dashing, like a fish,
　　' Oh! save me, John!' she cried;
' I would, my love—I wish it much,—
　　But you my hands have tied.'
　　　　　　　But you my hands have tied."

CHAPTER XVII.

PLEASANT HOURS.

IT was not to be expected that the Bemmidges should long remain ignorant of the arrival of Mr. Molozane and family at Stock Orchard Crescent.

Mr. Molozane was too often in Fen Court; Mr. Geith sat too often on the knife-boards of the Holloway omnibuses for shrewd conjectures not to be formed on the subject.

"Take my word for it," said Mr. Bemmidge, who never had been taken into the plot of marrying George to his sister-in-law, "that Geith has at last found a house where he can hang up his hat;" and this opinion, which the wine-merchant expressed gleefully, and to which the ladies listened in dismay, received confirmation on the following Sunday afternoon, when Mr. Geith was encountered

at Hornsey Rise, walking abroad with two young
ladies.

"As plain-looking a pair as you would desire to
meet," said Miss Gilling, with a snort, "and
dressed like Quakeresses. I should have thought
Mr. Geith would have been ashamed to be seen
out with such a couple of dowdies;" and Miss
Gilling, against whom the charge of simplicity
could not have been brought by anybody, tossed
her head disdainfully.

"They live in Stock Orchard Crescent," remarked Mrs. Bemmidge, "father and two daughters,
and are the people at whose house he spent so
much time the summer after he first came here."

"Well, there's no accounting for tastes," answered Gertrude. "I can only say neither of them
would be mine."

"Andrew says they have been great people,"
said Mrs. Bemmidge, thoughtfully.

"Andrew talks nonsense," snapped Miss Gilling,
and there was a pause after this frank observation.

"I was thinking of calling upon them," said Mrs.
Bemmidge, at length. "Andrew says, knowing
them has introduced Mr. Geith to a first-rate
business connection, and who knows but they

might do something for us? I am sure, with the children growing up, any person who could bring orders would be worth cultivating."

"I don't know who would give orders for blacking if they had to drink it," answered Miss Gilling. To which Mrs. Bemmidge replied:

"You-and mamma never refuse to take it, at any rate, when it is offered to you." A remark so undeniably true, that it induced Miss Gilling to turn the conversation.

"I wonder what kind of style they live in?" she said, ignoring her sister's last observation.

"You can see, if you like to call upon them with me," answered Mrs. Bemmidge; and the pair called accordingly upon Miss Molozane, greatly to Miss Molozane's astonishment.

Avowedly, they came as friends of Mr. Geith, and Beryl felt naturally a little disappointed in Mr. Geith's friends; but when once that gentleman had told her all he knew about them, she rested satisfied, and began taking amusement out of her new acquaintances, as she did out of everything else that came in her way.

Not an atom proud was my heroine. If the absence of pride be a fault, I am sorry for it; but she was not proud, nevertheless. Somehow she identified herself so little with her acquaintances; in her own mind, in her own hopes and happiness she stood so entirely aloof from those with whom she was thrown; knowing people was an affair so entirely outside of herself, that she never gave the matter of gentility a thought; poor though they might be, the Molozanes had always been *the* Hertfordshire Molozanes, and, as such, Molozanes with an assured station; and the old saying, that a cat may look at a king, holds equally true conversely—without any loss of dignity a king may look at a cat; and without any loss of caste in her own eyes, Beryl looked at the Bemmidges, took them for grist, and ground them up, for George Geith's delectation, in her ridicule mill.

From Mrs. Gilling to her youngest grandchild, Beryl could take off every turn of expression, every peculiarity of manner. She knew Mrs. Gilling's favourite preachers and platters of food, off by heart. She could tell to a nicety whether the dinner Mrs. Gilling had "dropped in" to partake of at her daughter's had pleased her or not, whether she had had her due share of the crackling, and if the stuffing had proved to her taste.

"I think they must live on pork," Louey observed. "We have never called there yet that there has not been an all-pervading smell of grease and onions. We stopped there once for "lunch," as Mrs. Bemmidge called it, but I will never stop again; Beryl may if she likes; I think she found her pudding very nice."

"So nice that Amy finished it," observed Beryl; "what nasty children they are. They would pick up pieces of pudding out of the cinders, I do think. I should like to have Amy here for a day, just to see what she would eat if she had her own will."

"I hate that child," said George, emphatically.

"That is ungrateful," observed Louey maliciously, "for she told us the other day she was very fond of you, and that you would be her uncle when you married Miss Gilling—oh! Beryl forgive me—I forgot. I did not mean to tell him—I did not indeed."

"You need not vex yourself about the matter," George answered, looking as he spoke at Beryl, who was laughing and blushing at one and the same time; "I shall certainly be the brat's uncle when I marry Miss Gilling, but that will be never."

"I should not like you if you married her," said Louey gravely. "I am afraid all friendship would be at an end between us."

"I shall not subject your friendship to so severe a test," George replied, amused in spite of his annoyance; "for I think Miss Gilling would as little suit me as I should suit her."

"Although she sings so beautifully?" said Beryl demurely.

"Beryl can sing so like her, that when I shut my eyes, I think it is Miss Gilling, and am afraid to smile," said Louisa. "She was here the other day squalling, and a little boy out in the street did one of her roulades after her so exactly, that Beryl had to go out of the room. I wish I could draw, Mr. Geith. I would give anything to be able to sketch Miss Gilling at the piano."

Whereupon the accountant sat down and produced a caricature of the young lady, curls and all, which would surely have delighted Miss Gilling, could she have seen it.

"I like that young man she is really going to marry," said Beryl, as George proceeded with his task, Louisa helping him by looking over his shoulder the while. "He is one of your clerks, is he not, Mr. Geith? Mr. Foss, I mean."

"Is Foss going to marry Miss Gilling?" asked George, pausing, and looking up with a sudden expression of displeasure.

"I do not know; I suppose so," stammered Beryl, who saw she had made a mistake somehow; "I think he must be going to marry her."

"Why do you think so?—that is, if I may ask such a question?"

"Because—because—how you do teaze one, Mr. Geith. I do not know why I think it, and besides I may be quite mistaken."

After which answer, spoken pettishly, Beryl relapsed into silence, and refused to laugh at Miss Gilling's portrait when it was finished.

We must be careful what we say to Mr. Geith about the Bemmidges," she remarked to her sister afterwards. "I hope I did not do any harm by what I told him. I wonder why he did not want Mr. Foss to marry 'Jurtrude?'" marvelled Beryl, mocking Mrs. Gilling's pronunciation of her daughter's name.

"I fancy I can guess," said Mr. Molozane, looking up from his newspaper, in which he had

not been so absorbed but that he could listen to his
daughters' conversation; "he thinks Miss Gilling
may learn too much about his business from Mr.
Foss, and I think he is very likely to be right; not
but what he is doing so well that I should have
imagined it could make little difference to him who
knew he was getting on."

"Is Mr. Geith rich then, papa?" asked Beryl.

"Not rich, but growing rich," was the reply; and
Mr. Molozane resumed his paper, whilst the girls
pursued their several occupations in silence.

The eldest was, as usual, engaged in needlework;
the youngest, according to custom, writing, for she
was strong again, and her family allowed her to
amuse herself in her own way, without let or
hindrance.

Sometimes, indeed, when her face got flushed,
and her hands began to tremble, Beryl would essay
to entice her from her manuscripts, but as Louisa
grew older she grew less manageable, and would
push her sister away, saying, with tears lying on
her cheeks:

"Go away, Beryl, you come between me and
them; I can't see them while you are standing
there."

"I wish you would not talk like that," Beryl sometimes ventured to expostulate.

"Talk like what? It is true; I do see everybody I write about a great deal plainer than I see you now. There, they are all gone; and what I had to say is gone. You have spoiled one of the best passages I ever wrote. I shall have to go to my own room if you do not leave me alone."

And at last, for very peace' sake, Beryl did leave her alone, and let her write verses to her heart's content.

Very gradually both father and sister were coming to understand that there is something stronger than parental authority, than affectionate solicitude; something which may lie in abeyance for a while, but which ultimately will have its own way—genius.

Almost in spite of themselves, a conviction forced itself on Mr. Molozane and Beryl, that the talent they had first ignored, and then striven to keep in swaddling clothes, was growing into a giant which should master them all.

"If your sister's health keep good," said George Geith to Beryl, one lovely summer's evening, when he overtook her in High Street, Islington, and they

walked home together to Stock Orchard Crescent,
"she will become a famous woman yet."

"But if her health should not keep good, Mr.
Geith," answered Beryl, "what fame would com-
pensate us for that?"

"She will write, in any case," was the reply, "so
you must hope for the best," an easy matter with
Beryl, who began from that time to build air
castles as to what Louise's genius was to do for
them. She knew she was not clever herself; she
knew there was nothing she did particularly well,
no one accomplishment in which she excelled ; so,
when once the idea took firm and full possession
of her, that Louey was going to achieve "great
things," she dwelt upon it in the sure conviction
that some day "papa would be able to rest again,
that Louey's verses would in the long run bring
her in a golden harvest."

Twelve months after they came to London, hope
began to have some tangible food on which to
exist.

Spite of Miss Gilling's strictures on their plainness, the two sisters were really very pretty girls,
and their blushing country faces gained them much
favour in the eyes of publishers.

There is not much gold lying about the base of the hill of fame; and Louisa Molozane, spite of her eager exertions, found none of the precious metal at all; but she got what was almost as good to her—praise, encouragement in the present, assurances of success in the future.

She had kindly notes from editors, favourable opinions from "readers," confirmatory smiles from publishers. Poems were not saleable articles, and tragedies could not be thought of; but still, "when she directed her attention to other branches of literature," "when she began to write short tales, for instance," there was no fear of failure. She had genius, she had youth. Let her read more and write less, said many a good-natured adviser, and she would yet be one of the first authoresses of the day.

Such was the sum and substance of a statement made to Beryl by an editor whom she had the happiness of seeing personally. At first he took her for the owner of the manuscript for which she called, and was more reticent of his remarks; but upon Beryl assuring him she could not write anything more ambitious than a letter, and that "not a long one," she added, he gave his opinion

x 2

in extenso, and sent the girl away so happy that she could have danced the whole way up to the top of the Caledonian Road, had she not feared scandalizing the passers-by.

By degrees also Mr. Molozane came to be associated with his daughter's literary efforts. He began by letting her repeat scraps of her verses as they sat in the firelight, or toiled in the summer twilight up Highgate Hill, or wandered through the green fields round about Hornsey and Crouch End, places that are almost built up to now, but which were then miles and miles away in the country.

In those days father and youngest born were so much together, that had Beryl been of a jealous temperament she might have thought herself hardly done by, but the girl never felt anything but thankfulness that "papa and Louey were so happy, that he was coming at last to understand her writing, and to like her doing it."

Out of the past there have been always a few things standing that have seemed unutterably pitiful, things that I have either seen myself, or that have come to my knowledge through others, and not the least pitiful appears the picture that now rises before me, of that poor, proud father wandering about London with a bundle of his daughter's manuscripts in his hand, manuscripts which were invariably returned to him unaccepted.

Often and often, as time went by, George Geith wondered how it would end, into what port the manuscripts now floating rudderless would drift at last, and whilst the Molozanes grew more eager, more confident, he became less satisfied about the probable result, and began to speculate whether Louisa's talent, though certain, might not be likewise unmarketable.

It was an idea he was not able to shake off. Till Mr. Molozane took the matter up, George had not troubled himself as to how it would all end; but he could not endure to see the ruined gentleman commence building such hopes on Louisa as he had built on the Sythlow Mines unless they were certain of fruition.

As he met Mr. Molozane hurrying off in his dinner-hour to the Row or the Strand; as he found him in the evenings carefully copying out Louisa's poems; when he saw the looks of pride the man was continually casting on the tall, slight girl who had so shot up since George Geith saw her, the accountant felt that disappointment would be something too terrible for them to face.

Often when he was talking to Beryl, he tried to discover whether the idea of failure had ever presented itself; but Beryl was so provokingly sanguine, that no doubts could be instilled into her; and it was so pleasant to him to listen to her hopeful chatter; her happy face seemed to her lover so lovely, that he never had the heart to tell her he considered the result of Louisa's labours problematical.

Happy days were those for all that little band— happy for father and daughters and for guest. There was no cloud on the horizon, no haunting dread in their minds, no sign of tempest in the sky; nothing had as yet occurred to trouble the peaceful current of their lives. There was no symptom of delicacy about Louisa now. Mr. Molozane seemed to be growing young again. Beryl looked a little weary perhaps at times, but what of that? George hoped soon to be able to take all responsibility off her shoulders. He was only waiting to propose formally until he had a certain sum in hand over and above the income he made annually out of figures. He had little fear but that ultimately

Beryl would listen favourably to his suit. He felt
sure Mr. Molozane would look kindly on him for a
son-in-law. At first he intended to take a house in
or near Stock Orchards Crescent, unless, indeed,
Beryl wished to remain under the same roof with
her father, in which case he would not cross her
inclination.

All the mad fever of fear and hopelessness was
over, and George Geith, the successful man of
business, merely waited the result of one or two
speculations before asking Beryl to be his wife.

It was then late in the autumn, and ere Christmas
he hoped to be visiting in Stock Orchard Crescent
as a future relative. He liked going there as a
friend ; but his heart throbbed joyfully at the anti-
cipation of something nearer, closer still.

He had worked for this ; he had been silent for
it ; and in the depths of his stern, reserved nature
lay the consciousness that in the sweat of his brow
he had expiated his former errors, and earned the
prospect of his present felicity.

Some memory of that past, some thought that
possibly a few particulars which could not be
inquired about by a friend, might be asked by a
future father-in-law, had perhaps contributed to a

certain tardiness in his suit. He had wanted to feel his footing certain before he ventured on another step; and now he mentally praised himself for his caution, and began to shape more tangibly the future of his life.

Even as the young authoress dreamt her dreams, so George Geith dreamt his; and as the time drew on for fruition to crown his hopes, happiness more swift-footed than he crossed the Molozanes' threshold, and brought acceptance of one of Louisa's often-rejected pieces to the family.

"To be sure it was not to be paid for, but the money is certain to follow," said the girl, with a little of her old air of sober wisdom; and she turned again to her writing-table to pen quires more poetry, on the strength of having disposed of four verses of rhyme.

"Money is certain to follow," repeated Solomon, after she had been writing for a long time; "it is a mere question of time," and she covered her happy face with her hands. "It is coming, Beryl; I feel it, and then shall we not do grand things? I am a little tired to-night; shall we build castles, Beryl? when I am a great authoress, where shall we live? when

I have a thousand pounds, what shall we do with it ?"

What would they not do? that was rather the question. A hundred thousand would not have bought all they mentally purchased, sitting in the firelight glow.

Molozane Park, or at least the Dower House; a house for papa; a pony phaeton for themselves; furniture *ad lib.*

" What colour should you like the drawing-room curtains ?" asked Louisa.

" We would have everything just as it used to be."

" Except that you would not mind setting a room aside for me and my rubbish, as you used to call it," laughed Louisa.

" I think I will give you a room when you make money enough to buy the house," answered Beryl.

" Wait a little longer," said Louisa, " and you shall see what you will see," and so, hand clasped in hand, they chattered on, seeing all things in the future, save the reality which was approaching them ; building all kinds of fancy habitations save those in which they were really to dwell.

Thinking of them, but children as they were, tracing out so fair a path, I am loath to tell of the roads they had separately to travel.

END OF VOL. II.